the exact likeness

of

living persons

Margaret J. McMaster

the exact likeness

of

living persons

Mansbridge Dunn Publishers

ISBN: 9781777170356

Cover design and sketches by Margaret J. McMaster

The author is a proud member of the
Writers' Union of Canada

Dedicated to my fabulous friends:
Gabriela, Kate, Sue, Claire, Ruth Ann,
Roz, Pauline, Annetta, Betty, and Eryl,
with whom I share a love of books,
tea and cakes,
and interesting conversations

ACKNOWLEDGMENTS

Effusive thanks to beta readers Sandy Cowan, Eryl Child, and Gabriela Pahl, for their insightful comments and corrections.

To my husband, Orland, you are a prince for taking care of the demanding Schnauzer while I worked.

And to my late mother, Jane (Baxter) Lawson, whose diaries provided the historical and personal context of the sole non-fiction piece, *What Was Left at the End* - you were the first writer.

CONTENT

etiquette

You waved to me from the ledge,
and self-conscious me never thought
of running to your rescue.
Only about the propriety of waving back.

end of a marriage

it peeled away like the skin
of a fish
in the heat of the pan
once taut as it
held the flesh together
swimming unmindful
until snagged
flipping and gasping
crossing over into ruin
with a fickle current
served with tartar sauce
and a wedge of lemon
cut from sweet white flesh
to be scraped into
the dog's bowl
and wolfed down
in one enthusiastic
gulp

the preacher

betrayed by the truth of his beliefs
having grown up as wild
and free as a horse
before it knows the bridle

scorned by his unanswered prayers
thundering across fields
of undulating grasses
the sun warming his back

shunned by the bread and wine
galloping without aim
across seven days of creation
with unhindered speed

choked by the starched collar
slouched sweaty and strained
slaking his thirst from the silver trough
held out to him by his master

The Answers

The right answer was churned out to sea
as the riptide sucked it under.

The wrong answer spewed upward like a fountain,
carrying baby birds closer to the sun.

The right answer weighed heavy under an eagle's talons.

The wrong answer bought beers for everyone at the pub.

The right answer crawled along the Galapagos shore
in the body of an ancient tortoise.

The wrong answer stepped into an open manhole
and emerged unscathed.

The right answer got lost in the unfathomable maze of
the desert.

The wrong answer pulled apart its entrails and feasted on
its eyeballs.

A House By the Sea

she looked for a down-and-out town
on the coast
one that tourism had ignored
devoid of historic buildings
and streets with curbs
with a small property she could
keep a pony on
one she could mount herself
and ride into town
a tiny house with a wood stove
and a well
with land and ocean
within view
a dog unafraid of the dark
to bark at wolves
near the chicken coop
the smell of the seasons
and salt air
and coffee on the stove
enough for this life

Morning Pages

The practice has its origins in *The Artist's Way* -
penning three pages, stream-of-consciousness,
first thing in the morning, to free the mind
for the serious business of writing.

It has a devoted following.
One advocate uses a particular brand of fountain pen
with turquoise ink and high-quality paper.
Another turns on a rock salt lamp and an oil-diffuser.

I don't know which is best. I'm new to the ritual,
trying to get past it before tackling my daily word count.
Wondering if it will electrify under-utilized brain synapses
and speed up the process.

I go with a fountain pen and dollar-store notebook,
forgoing a cup of coffee in case it's frowned upon,
then argue with myself about possible approaches.

Finally I give in and brew the coffee,
because I've got nothing.
The notebook is cracked open ready to go
but the pen is frozen at the starting line.
My brain is numb to everything except
letting the notebook blame the pen.

I peek at another author's Morning Pages online -
words of substance written in perfectly-punctuated
sentences.
A treatise on how life's tragedies can push us
to become who we are meant to be.

I rack my brain for a personal catastrophe
in order to plumb these depths
before the dog demands a walk.
Before I have to toast the bread and clean up the kitchen.
Before the plotline germinating in my head
finds another writer to attach itself to.

The fact that I'm failing at Morning Pages is unassailable.
I'm squeezed between the roaring demands of a work-in-
progress and the fear of ostracizing myself from a proven
method.
I can hardly breathe, let alone write.

The only way to keep the howling monster from blowing
my house down
is to improvise.

What evolves are not Morning Pages,
or Afternoon Pages,
or Evening Pages.
They are Anytime Pages.
Probably not three pages either.
A few paragraphs, perhaps, or a measly sentence.

Observations the universe has dropped
at my feet during the day.

Hosta leaves, newly pushed through the damp spring earth,
tightly curled and as green as a tomato hornworm.

Or snippets of research.

What happened at the Battle of the St. Lawrence.
The medicinal properties of Purple Dead Nettle.
Camp 60.
Anna Swan of Tatamagouche.

Important or irrelevant, I don't know.
It depends.

I like the flow of the fountain pen though.

Sadly Missed by his Family and Many Friends

None of the family were mentioned by name. *The survivors not wanting to be identified.* No funeral or visitation but a "family service" to be held later. She wondered what that would entail. Champagne cocktails as they flushed his ashes down the toilet?

The online guestbook was illuminating though. Polite notes from business colleagues and clients. An unknown woman overcome by grief. Sympathy extended to the surviving wives and children. Nothing from the children he'd pitted against each other since birth (*Finally, a boy!*), who were well aware of their uneven inheritances.

Family. It was like a dog he kept chained in the backyard. If anyone asked him if he had a dog he would describe it in the most glowing terms, including how much he loved it. But the dog was still chained up in the yard. It was a comfort to him, knowing it was there, but the truth was that he was the main force behind its suffering and he chose not to alleviate it.

They weren't stupid women, the two he married. The latest, her sister, was twenty years his junior, so inexperienced with men that she hadn't understood the motive behind the seduction: that he'd mapped her out as a breeder with a respectable gene pool, able to provide him with a more brilliant and accomplished set of children. Someone unlikely to balk at repeated pregnancies until she delivered a male to immortalize his name. *Her guilt over introducing the two of them was ongoing.*

His son's arrival released him from his marriage's narrative. Hardly anyone knew what his wife looked like anyway because he rarely appeared in public with her. Unable to account for his coolness, she privately rebuked herself for what had gone wrong.

His in-laws thought they'd offended him in some way, unaware of the restless passions that were decidedly less of a strain than a houseful of relatives. To anyone who asked, he explained himself in black and white terms: his number one priority was work; his number two priority was recovering from work. And certainly no one could fault him for his achievements or say that he wasn't a good provider. It was just that his comfort zone lay within very tight boundaries.

The cause of death was not specified and difficult to determine from the obituary. A mention of where to send donations would have been helpful.

His associates pictured a protracted end-of-life scenario, like the painful rotting of his internal organs, or a slow bleed-out from a knife wound. *Crying out for his mother as he wound down.* The tactful wording suggested suicide to some and was given credence by the absence of a funeral. (No probing questions to be asked or answered.) Except that no one could imagine what reason he'd have to escape such a self-involved life.

Some people knew how he'd died, of course. His wives and children. The coroner. Her.

He died on a beautiful day in late October, a postscript to a stifling summer.

She was working when he called, papers piled in mounds on the pine table, all the windows open in the loft. A grinding pain was radiating into her neck from the tight, twisted muscles in her shoulders and she wanted a break. So did he, apparently. A few hours off for a brisk walk at the Marsh and a perch dinner afterwards, if she liked. She asked why he wanted her to go instead of his wife, *as if that was likely*, and he told her that the children were sick with stomach flu.

Punishing heat and humidity had kept her inside the past few months and she was hungry for fresh air and exercise. Midweek, this time of year, the Conservation Area would be deserted, birders and tourists long gone, the entrance unsupervised. It was entirely doable.

She pulled the homemade granola bars she'd been keeping for such an occasion out of the freezer, figuring they'd thaw on the drive out, and packed her binoculars in case something interesting was left behind after the fall migration.

The parking lot was empty except for his BMW. She parked a discreet distance away and looked for him. He wasn't visible in her line of sight so she started down the trail. It cut beside a field of harvested corn before redirecting itself onto the grassy dyke that wound through the marsh. All around her were pale greens and tans, soft blues and greys, a colour palette she'd used when decorating her condo.

At last she saw him, field glasses up to his face, concentrating on two Cattle Egrets in the midst of the reeds. Her approach startled them and he followed the arc of their ascension from water into air.

He stepped forward to embrace her but she stepped back and the gesture dropped awkwardly into the space between them.

'Why did you set off before I got here?' she wanted to know.

He'd miscalculated and was annoyed. 'Let's get going, shall we?' he said, taking long strides forward, leaving her behind.

'Hold on, Paul Bunyan,' she called after him. 'I didn't come down here to race five k.'

He reconsidered and slowed his pace.

Anyone would have assumed that he was the more athletic of the two of them, but by the time they reached the first lookout he was barely keeping up.

'What's the matter with you?'

He paused to catch his breath. 'I think I'm going to die.'

'No kidding. Aren't we all.'

'I'm not joking.'

Had he had some sort of premonition?

'You mean, today?'

He shrugged as they headed up the lookout's wooden steps.

'What brought this on? Are you sick?' He was certainly a candidate for any number of Type A catastrophes.

He shook his head. 'It was like a dream. Kübler-Ross. The whole nine yards. I was there and back in an instant.'

He'd never spoken of anything even remotely spiritual before and she'd assumed it was because he couldn't contemplate any other gods before him.

She slapped his arm in jest as they reached the top. 'Stop it. You're killing me.'

He sat on the bench that ran the perimeter of the platform and stretched out his legs. 'I was there,' he said solemnly, 'leaving my body, travelling towards the white light.'

'When was this?'

'Just before you arrived.'

'You were sitting in your car and you dozed off?'

'No, I was dead! Floating into the afterlife!'

'And then you rose again?' she scoffed.

He gave her a sour look. 'I held onto the silver thread. A woman was there and I asked her if I could go back. She looked at me as though it was obvious, but I couldn't see that it was. And then I started sliding down the thread, back into my body.'

Suddenly she spied a Bald Eagle perched high in a tree, waiting for some prey to expose itself. 'You're not taking LSD again, are you?' she said as she pulled up her binoculars.

'What? No!'

'What then?'

'Nothing, I swear.'

The eagle was magnificent. She couldn't take her eyes off it. It was a small thing silhouetted against the expansive landscape, but powerfully dominating. She tried to make the moment last.

He was glumly ruminating on his moments in the afterlife when she pulled the granola bars out of her pocket and gave him half.

'I made them myself,' she explained, 'so there's nothing but the good stuff in them.'

He thanked her for her thoughtfulness and smiled for the first time that afternoon. It was a smile that had once drawn her in.

Romance was the furthest thing from his mind though. She could see that. He was petrified. Afraid, that despite all the careful constructs of his life, he'd be leaving it early. And not sure that what was waiting for him would be enough to satisfy his appetites.

She observed that the sky was darkening and the wind was picking up. 'I think the day's about to turn nasty.'

'They weren't predicting rain,' he replied, 'but this close to the lake, you never know.'

They chewed in silence while a Long-Billed Dowitcher poked around the mud flats. A few weeks in the fridge and the granola bars were still perfectly edible and quite delicious. He ate his share before his heart started pounding wildly and his tongue bloated into the caverns of his mouth. A certain realization hit him. *Or was it resignation?*

'You ...' he whispered as his airways choked off his breath, 'did ... you ...'

'Of course not,' she replied truthfully as the Dowitcher flew off.

When she saw that the time for worrying about the life ever after was over, she dabbed the corners of her mouth and folded the plastic bag neatly into her jacket pocket. A flock of Canada Geese, haunted by the memory of migration, heralded his exit across the sky like a hundred trumpets.

She left him there and made her way back to the car. No sooner was she on the road than a furious rain started hammering the windshield, a phenomenon she attributed to "lake effect".

Rush hour was still hours away and traffic was light. When she got back to the city she pulled into the SuperStore and called her sister to see if there was anything she needed. She, herself, had run out of peanut oil.

Her sister wept with gratitude and fatigue.

'You're an angel. The kids have been throwing up all day and I haven't been able to leave the house.'

'Don't worry, pet,' she said as she dumped the bag of crumbs into the trash can by the entrance. 'Everything's going to be all right.'

Then she stepped forward and waited for the automatic doors to open.

She Should Have Known

She was combing through the closet looking for clues.
The relationship was new and she was unsure of it.
Of him.
Something felt a bit off and she didn't know
if it was a reliable instinct.
Maybe it was a cell memory from a previous
relationship. A revelation that made her question
every word he'd ever said to her.

It was a dream, actually, the thing that set it off.
A dream where she'd walked in on him during
an intimate embrace with another woman
and he'd looked at her with disdain.
As though she was doing something wrong,
not him.

Was it a side of him that he kept hidden?
Something she would have noticed if
she hadn't been so besotted with love?

Or was it love? Some guidebooks would say no,
it was infatuation –
not uncommon in the early stage of a relationship
when a man is still making eye contact and
putting his hand on a woman's back as they
slip into a restaurant.

He hadn't actually said I love you, but he was,
she thought, the kind of guy who let things play
out naturally.

Or was she wrong? Was he reticent because he
was still attached to a former love?
Was it the woman they ran into at the park?
A woman with a certain air of mystery about her.
Did she have information, secrets?
Was she thinking: I know something you don't know?

It was over, he said. O.V.E.R.
She didn't belabour the point because he looked
sincere, and it could be true. Or not.
It was hard enough admitting your own truth.
She'd never told anyone hers. It was buried
so deep an archaeologist couldn't find it.

The clothes hung tightly packed in his closet.
His taste ran to cargo pants and brilliant white t-shirts.
Smart dress pants and Polo shirts for work.
She had to pull them out and lay them on the bed
in order to check for receipts for gifts
he'd never given her.

She judged the time it would take him to run
to the bridge and back and had replaced
everything where it belonged
when he reappeared and pressed

her against his sweaty chest.
She squealed in mirthful protest as
he bruised his salty lips against hers.

She had an early meeting, she said as she grabbed
her purse. He thought they'd have breakfast together
and was disappointed. Or was it feigned?
He did seem surprised at the abruptness of her
departure but said he would call her later.
Maybe they could grab a bite to eat after work.

They wouldn't, of course.
She was out the door, having fanned every
book for a forgotten love letter, checked the
bathroom cabinet for tampons, swept under
the bed for misplaced hair clips.
There was nothing. Nothing suspicious. Nothing
incriminating.

Which meant that he could be exactly what he
appeared to be: a decent guy. Honest, reliable.
Straight out of a Cosmo survey about
what every woman wants.

And now, the only way to properly love him,
was to lose him. To sever all communication before
she had to witness the warty monster inside her
consume the sugar of his soul. Before he made her
happy and then took it back.

What Was Left at the End

Imagine that the boys in your life wear suits to church and stand when you enter a room. They don't wait for the draft but sign up right after the Air Force recruiter delivers his pitch to your city, which happens to be Windsor, Ontario. You're eighteen, and the tall, lanky boy you've started dating is twenty. He's quit his job and is getting fitted for his uniform.

The miniscule diary entries for 1941 give me eyestrain, even when I'm using a magnifying glass. Transcribing seventy-one years of my mother's life for the rest of the family is a tricky process.

I was born in 1950, before society and the way it works had changed very much. I remember the essence of those days. Still, my friends weren't swept up and disposed of by war.

My imagination struggles with this: a man barely out of high school responsible for a plane full of men and bombs, the way it happened to my mother's boyfriend, Gooch.

1941
Tues., Feb. 18. Cleaned house. Went to school this aft. Tea dance, war–savings stamps. Grandpa & Grandma, Uncle Harry, Aunt Hilda, Rawsie came. Asked Gooch to K– Hop. He asked me to his house Saturday night.

Mon. June 30. Hot again. Gooch & Tickie left. Johnny Mills called & talked to me. Went back to work & worked until 12:00 and was it ever hot. Mom & Dad picked me up.

Sun. July 6. Gooch in Sarnia. Herb called at 10:15. Came right out & stayed till one. Went to Sansburn's for a chicken dinner. We went to Coulter's for a swim but I didn't go in – too cold.

The first tragedy strikes when a Nazi night fighter crosses the English Channel and kills Gooch's older brother, a Spitfire pilot.

Mon. July 7. Wrote Liz an 8 page letter. It rained. Gooch's brother killed in England. Wrote Gooch & Herb & Jack letters. Went to Betty's. We planned our trip to Toronto over Aug. 4.

Sun. July 20. Grandma & Grandpa stayed all night. Took them to Amherstburg, also Bern. Went to Kingsville. Took Grandma & Grandpa to Pearl's. Bern & I picked up Puss & Mills. Fed them. Went for a ride. Puss bought the gas.

On October 23rd, mother asks Gooch's younger brother, John, nicknamed Puss, to accompany her to a Roundabout and discovers that he's been called to report to the Air Force that night. She now works at the same bank he does, a job her high school principal found for her because she couldn't afford university.

Fri. Oct. 24. Not very busy. Proved my ledger. Mr. Higgins mad at Puss for enlisting. He & I took stuff over to his mother. Then went to Roundabout at Masonic & Hip Hop at Walkerville. Herb called about 11.

Sat. Oct. 25. Not terribly busy but I didn't get out until 2:45. Puss's last day. Met Betty & we went to see "A Yank in the R.A.F.". Called Mom. Puss had called saying Gooch & Tick were in London & were on their way home. Called back to say Tick was alone. Wrote Gooch & Liz. Bed by 9:30.

Mon. Oct. 27. Rainy & ate lunch here. Balanced my ledger 1st shot. Betty picked me up. Wickham's at our place for dinner. Registered at Night School. Went to Howie's. Puss accepted in R.C.A.F. Went to Bellvue. Letters from Gooch & Marg. Wrote to Gooch.

At the end of 1942, after training has ended and the hometown boys have been shipped overseas, the social life changes.

1942
Thurs. Nov. 5. Busy with Victory Loan. Marj picked me up for Miss Canada meeting. Got candy etc. for a box. Washed my hair.

Fri. Nov. 6. Marj wanted me to go to Detroit. Didn't go. Worked till 6. Troops arrived in England. Baxter's came down. Mailed box.

Mother and her friends knit socks, write long letters, and mail packages containing cigarettes and chocolate. Several black and white movies are released each week and they go to all of them. They're double features of war or romance and sometimes a mixture of the two - no sex or swearing, offensive or otherwise, just passionate kisses and misunderstandings that must be cleared up.

1943
Mon. Jan. 18. Tired all day. Sent Gooch & Jack parcels. Lost ration books. Looked high & low for them.

Fri. Sept. 24. Went to show right after dinner with Liz & Marg. Saw "Mr. Lucky" – Cary Grant & Loraine Day. Very good. Went to Jackson Park & Honey Dew after.

Sat. Oct. 30. Two airgraphs from Gooch. Went to dance at Service Club as a clown. It was horrible. One of 6 chosen for funniest costume.

My mother's family grows a Victory Garden but food shortages aren't affecting Canada the way they are Great Britain. Radio and newspapers provide the only information about what the boys, now men, are accomplishing overseas. But exactly where they are stationed is unknown.

As anyone at home waiting for a shred of information knows, "missing" is often a precursor to much worse news. Thankfully, my mother's brother, Jack, now a captain, is located in a German P.O.W. camp, his batman having made a wrong turn in France that landed them at a farmhouse full of Germans.

Then, word arrives that Gooch is missing.

Thurs. Nov. 11. John phoned from London. Gooch missing. How can it be true? Called Marg in Toronto. Dad went to London with me. Puss & Tick home. Mrs. Newton there. Talked till 11:00.

Gooch was a bomber pilot, on loan to the British Air Force, flying raids out of Nigeria. On November 6th, he and his crew of four Britons and one Australian were looking for targets to bomb and discovered a German warship off the coast of Greece. They dropped sixteen bombs and sank it but were bombarded with flak, some of which hit one of the Wellington's engines. It functioned long enough for them to get clear and when it conked out Gooch ditched the plane flawlessly into the sea.

For the next ten days the starving people on the island of Sifnos hid the airmen in a mountaintop monastery and took up precious fruit and cheese to keep them alive. The mayor vowed they wouldn't be captured and arranged for a fisherman to take them to the island of Serifos in the dead of night. There they discovered five British commandos spying on German troop movements from a goat pen dug into a cave. The Brits had a wireless and were able to organize a rescue.

Twenty days later a Royal Navy gunboat disguised as a Greek fishing vessel picked them up and transferred them to safety in Cyprus. Gooch's harrowing ordeal was over.

Fri., Nov. 26. Gooch safe – was missing after raid on Greece. Peggy Barr called. Called Mrs. Martin & Mrs. Duck. Washed my hair. Bed early.

Wed. Dec. 8. Ottawa phoned Gooch's mother. "Crew back at base." Wrote him. I.O.D.E. meeting at Dinny's. Sewed.

Thurs. Dec. 9. Cable from Gooch. "Back in circulation. Real experience. Please cable. Writing. Love." Cable him "Overjoyed with news. Curiosity is killing me. All my love." Night School. So happy again.

When Gooch returned to base, he was handed a cable informing him that his father, a physician working for the war effort in London, Ontario, had dropped dead the week before he left on his mission.

Fri. Dec. 10. Two more letters from Gooch sent Nov. 3rd & 6th. Didn't know about his father. Wrote him. Jessie called. Talked quite a while. Have a cold. Hot bath. Bed early. Wrote Gooch's mother.

Gooch was flown back to Canada in February of 1944 and served the remainder of the war as a trainer at the RCAF station in Comox, British Columbia.

Puss, who'd also become a bomber pilot, was shot down in a raid over Hanover, Germany a few months before the war in Europe ended.

With his two brothers and father dead, Gooch moved to Toronto to be near his mother's family. He married and had three children and became a successful businessman.

My brothers and I grew up with Gooch and his family as part of our lives, aware that he'd once been my mother's boyfriend. He remained a dashing figure, a man of liberal viewpoints who liked to throw a provocative question into a dinner party and watch the fur fly.

In different circumstances the romance with my mother might have continued after he was decommissioned, although the diaries reflect a relationship conducted almost entirely in absentia, through letters and longing and needing each other to get through it all. Their friendship, and no doubt the memories, survived the following decades until they died in their eighties.

The escape of Flight Lieutenant Robert Adams, a.k.a. Gooch, and his crew, was the subject of a 1966 CBC documentary.

Gooch's father, Dr. Frederick Adams, was Windsor's first Medical Officer of Health.

HAZEL & HENRY

A Play in Three Acts —

*in which it is demonstrated that love
in old age is a complicated affair.*

Synopsis

Hazel Beecham has one objective before she dies: to get herself a boyfriend, and Amber, the precocious girl who cleans her room at the Peach Gardens Retirement Home, has no trouble fixing her up with likely prospects. Overlooking their flaws is another matter though, one that Hazel must come to terms with if she's to find true love.

Character Breakdown

Hazel Beecham: early 80s, a widow, residing at the Peach Gardens Retirement Home;

Officer Windham: mid-50s, the police officer who questions Hazel about an incident she was party to at the bank;

Kevin Beecham: mid-40s Hazel's son, good-hearted but preoccupied;

Amber: 16 years old, the girl who cleans Hazel's room;

Shirley Townsend: early 80s, Hazel's best friend since childhood;

Dr. Oliver: mid-50s, the physician who attends to the residents at the Home;

Dr. Komar: mid-30s, a neurology resident assigned to Dr. Oliver;

Henry: early 80s, a bachelor who has travelled the world and is interested in Hazel;

Nurse: late 40s, on staff at the Home;

Sally: late 40s, a volunteer from the Women's Institute who visits the residents;

Marie: mid-40s, Hazel's longtime hairdresser;

Victor Branch: late 20s, a young man with a shady past;

Carlos: mid-30s, an attendant at the DELTACARE Long Term Care facility.

ACT I

Scene 1

SETTING: The interrogation room of a police station, equipped with a table, two chairs, and a two-way mirror.

AT RISE: HAZEL is timidly looking around the room when OFFICER WINDHAM enters.

OFFICER WINDHAM

Mrs. Beecham? I'm Officer Windham. How are you doing today?

HAZEL

Fine, thank you.

OFFICER WINDHAM

If you don't mind, I'd like to ask you a few questions about the incident at the bank.

HAZEL

Okay.

OFFICER WINDHAM

Please sit down.

HAZEL

All right.
(sits down)

OFFICER WINDHAM

As a matter of record, would you please state your name and where you reside.

HAZEL

My name is Hazel Beecham and I live at the Peach Gardens Retirement Home.

OFFICER WINDHAM

How long have you lived at that address?

HAZEL
(thinking)

I'm not sure.

OFFICER WINDHAM

Were you living there when the incident occurred?

HAZEL
(shaking her head)
No, I wasn't. They put me there after it happened.

OFFICER WINDHAM

Who put you there?

HAZEL

My son, Kevin, and his wife. They thought I was becoming a handful.

OFFICER WINDHAM

Were you living with them at the time?

HAZEL

Yes. I just can't remember what day it was.

OFFICER WINDHAM

It was April 15th.

HAZEL

I already told one of your people what happened.

OFFICER WINDHAM

Yes, I know. Would you mind going over it one more time for me?

HAZEL

If you like.

OFFICER WINDHAM
Had you intended on going to the bank that day?

HAZEL
No. I only go when I need to use the bank machine.

OFFICER WINDHAM
What happened that made you go?

HAZEL
A man came to the door. Kevin and his wife were at work.

OFFICER WINDHAM
Why was he at your door?

HAZEL
(thinking hard)
I don't know.

OFFICER WINDHAM
Did he come into the house?

HAZEL
(wild-eyed, with a whispered, frantic
tone to her voice as she remembers)
Yes. He pushed his way in.

OFFICER WINDHAM

Did he hurt you?

HAZEL

(the words come as quick as the memories)

Yes! He grabbed my arm and twisted it until I fell to my knees. Then he bent down and hissed in my ear.

OFFICER WINDHAM

What did he say?

HAZEL

He said he wanted money. He told me he'd kill me if I didn't give it to him.

OFFICER WINDHAM

What did you do?

HAZEL

(upset to the point of tears)

I gave him what was in my purse but he said it wasn't enough and slapped me hard across the face.

OFFICER WINDHAM

Take your time, Mrs. Beecham. Did he have a weapon?

HAZEL

Yes, he had a gun.

OFFICER WINDHAM

Did you see the gun?

HAZEL
(shaking her head)
No. He was pushing it into my ribs while we were waiting for
the teller.

OFFICER WINDHAM

Why were you waiting for the teller when there's a bank
machine outside?

HAZEL

I thought there was a better chance he'd get caught if I could
get him into the bank.
(looking very satisfied with herself)

OFFICER WINDHAM

And how did you do that?

HAZEL

I told him I had lots of money, more money than he'd ever
need for the rest of his life, and that I'd get it for him if he
didn't kill me.

OFFICER WINDHAM

And did you?

HAZEL

Did I what?

OFFICER WINDHAM

Have lots of money?

HAZEL

Not gobs of it. I just wanted to get him into the bank.

OFFICER WINDHAM

Tell me what happened when you got up to the teller.

HAZEL

She asked if she could help me and I screamed, "HELP! HE'S GOT A GUN! HELP ME!"

OFFICER WINDHAM

You yelled even though he had a gun pressed to your ribs?

HAZEL
(defensively)

What else could I do?

OFFICER WINDHAM

You could have been killed. Was the money more important than your life?

HAZEL

Are you saying that my life is important?

OFFICER WINDHAM

Isn't it?

HAZEL

No one I know considers it important. But the money is all I have to leave Kevin when I die.

OFFICER WINDHAM

What happened after you screamed?

HAZEL

He wasn't expecting that and he ran like a scared rabbit.

OFFICER WINDHAM

What did the staff do?

HAZEL

Nothing! The teller just stood there! No one was doing anything and he was getting away!

OFFICER WINDHAM

So you ran after him?

HAZEL
(agitated)

He was getting away!

OFFICER WINDHAM

Did he know you were running after him?

HAZEL

I don't think so. He didn't look back. He just jumped into his car.

OFFICER WINDHAM

And how did you respond to that?

HAZEL

I jumped spreadeagle onto the trunk and held on for dear life.

OFFICER WINDHAM
(raising an eyebrow)

What were you hoping to accomplish with that move?

HAZEL

(voice rising)

I THOUGHT SOMEONE MIGHT THINK A LITTLE OLD LADY HANGING ONTO THE TRUNK OF A CAR WAS A LITTLE UNUSUAL AND CALL THE POLICE!

OFFICER WINDHAM

You could have been seriously injured.

HAZEL

(considerably wound up)

I COULD HAVE BEEN SHOT DEAD IN THE BANK! AT LEAST THIS WAY HE'S NOT GOING TO BE ABDUCTING OTHER LITTLE OLD LADIES, IS HE?

(There's a knock at the door. OFFICER WINDHAM opens it. Another officer motions him into the hallway. KEVIN BEECHAM is standing there.)

OFFICER WINDHAM

Mr. Beecham? What can I do for you?

KEVIN

I think my mother is at the tipping point for someone in her condition. She's becoming way too agitated.

OFFICER WINDHAM
Is she? I thought she was holding up rather well.

KEVIN
She's more delicate than she appears. I'm afraid she's working herself into a state.

OFFICER WINDHAM
Very well. I think I have enough for now.

KEVIN
Good.

(OFFICER WINDHAM goes back into the room.)

OFFICER WINDHAM
We're finished with the interview now, Mrs. Beecham.

HAZEL
You don't want to ask me any more questions?

OFFICER WINDHAM
Not at this time. (looking at his watch)
Let the record show that this interview is being terminated at 3:23 p.m..
(gathers his papers and stands)
I'll show you out.

(BLACKOUT)

(END OF SCENE)

ACT 1

Scene 2

SETTING: Early morning. Hazel's cozy room at the Peach Gardens Retirement Home. The room has a TV and two comfortable chairs facing each other with a coffee table in the centre. There is a small kitchenette with an electric kettle and bar fridge under the counter. To one side is a bed and night table. There is an emergency pull cord beside the bed. A door leads to a bathroom.

AT RISE: HAZEL is buttoning her cardigan as AMBER steps out of the bathroom.

AMBER
(jovially)
I would have helped you with that, Mrs. B. It's all part of the service.

HAZEL
I can do it. My hands are pretty good today.

AMBER
(straightening up Hazel's bed)
You've only got a few minutes to get down to breakfast. As soon as I get the bed made up I'll walk you down.

HAZEL

That won't be necessary, Amber. Shirley's picking me up.

AMBER

Good enough, Mrs. B. You're lucky to have a BFF.

HAZEL

She's not my BFF. She's my bosom buddy.

AMBER

Bosom buddy? I guess that would make you BBFs.

HAZEL
(looking AMBER over)
You've got a nice bosom. I did too when I was your age.

AMBER

They're called knockers now, Mrs. B.

HAZEL

Knockers? What do you mean? Like door knockers?

AMBER

Or racks. Sometimes they're called racks.

HAZEL

Why?

AMBER

Who knows? It's a whole new world out there.

HAZEL

One I'll not be sorry to leave.

AMBER
(shaking her head)
We've had this conversation before, Mrs. B. You've got to stop thinking like that.

HAZEL

Why, because I've got so much to live for? How do I know one of those fellows you keep setting me up with won't slip a date rape drug into my drink?

AMBER

All the gents have been nice men, haven't they Mrs. B? None of them would stoop that low.

HAZEL

Stoop? The last one could barely walk.

AMBER

Archie?
(HAZEL nods)
What do you expect? He's waiting for a hip replacement!

HAZEL

Which makes him no good for dancing.

AMBER

Dancing? When did that get on the list?

HAZEL

Since that interminable bore, Rodney. I didn't know what to do
with him.

AMBER

You can just talk to them, Mrs. B. You don't have to go all Fred
Astaire and Ginger Rogers right off the bat.

HAZEL

I just think you could screen the candidates a little better.

AMBER
(sputtering)

Candidates! What candidates? It's slim pickin's out there, you
know.

HAZEL

Is it? Muriel What's-Her-Name seems to have dinner with a
new man every night.

                    AMBER

Maybe she puts out.

                    HAZEL

What?

                    AMBER

Never mind. Listen, Mrs. B, tonight's set-up is a slam dunk.
Guaranteed.

                    HAZEL
                  (skeptical)
Oh, really. What's he like?

                    AMBER
                  (teasing)
He's very sexy, with smouldering blue eyes.

                    HAZEL

My husband had blue eyes.

                    AMBER

So did Paul Newman. My aunt ran into him, you know ...
literally ran into him as he was coming out of the King Edward
Hotel. That's what she said about him: his eyes were the bluest
blue she'd ever seen.

HAZEL

If his eyes are his best feature he must be a real dog.

AMBER

(startled)

Who? Paul Newman?

HAZEL

No, this guy you're sending around tonight.

AMBER

Henry. His name's Henry, Mrs. B. Please don't eat him on the first date.

HAZEL

As long as he doesn't smell like pizza, he'll be safe. I've been dying for a pizza ever since I moved in here.

AMBER

I told him to come around for drinks at quarter to eight.

HAZEL

(sarcastically)

I hope he likes Ensure.

AMBER

Just make him a cup of tea, Mrs. B. And talk to him. He won't bite.

HAZEL

The Home isn't going to make a big fuss, is it?

AMBER

Not a bit. There's a skeleton staff at that hour and most of the residents are watching Jeopardy.

(There's a knock at the door.)

HAZEL

That must be Shirley.

AMBER

Got it, Mrs. B. You run along for your toast and scrambled eggs. I'll finish up here.

HAZEL

(turning back to AMBER as she opens the door)
Quarter to eight, you said?

AMBER

That's right, Mrs. B.

(HAZEL exits the room and closes the door behind her. She and SHIRLEY walk down the hall.)

SHIRLEY

Who were you talking to?

HAZEL

Amber.

SHIRLEY

Oh. What's happening at quarter to eight?

HAZEL

(shaking her head)

Another one of her disastrous hook-ups.

SHIRLEY

(stops and looks at HAZEL)

Honestly, Hazel, I don't know why you think you have to have a man at your age. What are they good for?

HAZEL

Why shouldn't I have a boyfriend? What's the harm in it?

SHIRLEY

Don't be defensive. I only meant …

HAZEL
What? That I'm too old? That it's too late for me?

SHIRLEY
(rethinking her position)
Sorry. You're absolutely right. It doesn't hurt anyone.

HAZEL
(satisfied)
Good. I couldn't stand it if you thought I wasn't worth a bit of
fun and companionship.

SHIRLEY
(putting her arm through hers)
Don't worry, sweetie. Your secret's safe with me.

(BLACKOUT)

(END OF SCENE)

ACT 1

Scene 3

SETTING: Clinic examination room at the Peach Gardens Retirement Home.

AT RISE: DR. OLIVER is leaning against a desk examining a chart when DR. KOMAR enters.

DR. KOMAR

Dr. Oliver?
(DR. OLIVER collects himself as DR. KOMAR reaches out his hand)
I'm Dr. Komar, your new resident.
(shaking hands)
I can't tell you what an honour it is to work with you, sir.

DR. OLIVER
(nodding modestly)
Glad to have you on board, Komar. You're right on time.

DR. KOMAR
(jovially)
Don't know how. I kept punching Peach Orchards instead of Peach Gardens into the GPS. By all rights I should be in Georgia!

DR. OLIVER
(dryly)
Yes, well, our first patient is Mrs. Hazel Beecham.
(He hands DR. KOMAR her chart.)
Mrs. Beecham has early Parkinson's Disease. She's taking part
in the clinical trial for MagnaDopa.

DR. KOMAR
MagnaDopa. I've heard of it. How's she getting along?

(There's a knock at the door.)

DR. OLIVER
There she is. You can ask her yourself.

(HAZEL enters.)

HAZEL
(eyeing DR. KOMAR)
Oh, you're new.

DR. OLIVER
Yes, Dr. Komar is a neurology resident. He'll be working with
me for a while.

DR. KOMAR

Very nice to meet you, Mrs. Beecham.

(Hazel positions herself on the examining table.)

I see you know the drill.

HAZEL

Please, call me Hazel. I'm not fussy about the Mrs. Beecham thing.

DR. KOMAR

Hazel it is, then.

DR. OLIVER

I'm just going to listen to your heart, Mrs. Beecham.

(He takes his stethoscope and listens carefully, then puts it down.)

Would you mind holding your hands out in front of you, like this.

(HAZEL extends her arms and holds them steady.)

Good. You can put them down now. How are you doing with the MagnaDopa? You mentioned you had dry eyes the last time I saw you.

HAZEL

(cheerily)

All cleared up now, thanks to the eye drops you prescribed.

DR. OLIVER

Any other problems? Constipation? Headaches?

HAZEL

No, I haven't experienced anything like that.

DR.OLIVER
(steps back and motions to DR. KOMAR)
Please continue the examination, Dr. Komar.

DR. KOMAR

My pleasure.
How long have you had Parkinson's, Hazel?

HAZEL

I noticed it just after I moved in here.

DR. KOMAR

You started having tremors?

HAZEL

Yes. At first I hardly noticed them, but then I had trouble holding onto things.

DR. KOMAR

Dr. Oliver tells me that you're taking part in the MagnaDopa trial.

HAZEL

That's right.

DR. KOMAR

Have your tremors changed since you've been on the drug?

HAZEL

Very much so. I can hold a cup of tea without flinging it all over myself.

DR. KOMAR

Excellent. What about mood swings? Have you been depressed or weepy?

HAZEL

I *was* depressed when I first moved here, but that was before I went on the MagnaDopa. The place doesn't bother me as much now.

DR. KOMAR

So, you've settled in. That's good. What activities do you take part in?

HAZEL

Activities?

DR. KOMAR

Yes, are you into bingo or exercise class?

HAZEL

I don't ... I'm not the type of person who mingles. It takes me a
long time to make friends.

DR. KOMAR

I see. Are you sleeping all right? Do you take a sleeping pill?

HAZEL
(reluctantly)

No.

DR. KOMAR

Why did you hesitate?

HAZEL

Well, it's going to sound crazy.

DR. KOMAR

That doesn't matter. What is it?

HAZEL

When I close my eyes at night, I see triangles.

DR. KOMAR

Triangles?

HAZEL

Yes, triangles, in different colours. They flit all over the place.
It's like looking through a kaleidoscope. But then I fall asleep
and … well, that's all there is to it, really.

DR. KOMAR

Anything else? Any scary nightmares?

HAZEL

No. I sleep like a top.

DR. KOMAR

A what?

HAZEL

Never mind.

DR. OLIVER
(interjecting)

Thank you, Mrs. Beecham.
(She gets off the examining table.)
I'm glad you're doing so well. If you have any concerns before
your next visit, be sure to let the duty nurse know.

HAZEL

I will, Dr. Oliver. I try to stay on the good side of everyone.

DR. KOMAR

Nice meeting you, Hazel.

HAZEL

You too.

(HAZEL exits. DR. OLIVER starts entering notes on her chart.)

DR. KOMAR

The coloured triangles ... she's having hypnagogic hallucinations.

DR. OLIVER

Yes. They're not uncommon with this class of drug.

DR. KOMAR

Are you going to change her dosage?

DR. OLIVER
(dismissively)

I don't think that's necessary. Still, we've got to document every side effect scrupulously for the trial.

                    DR. KOMAR
                     (nodding)
Of course.

(There's a knock at the door.)

                    DR. OLIVER
That will be our next patient.

(BLACKOUT)

(END OF SCENE)

ACT 1

Scene 4

SETTING: Evening. Hazel's room.

AT RISE: HAZEL and her son, KEVIN, enter.

HAZEL
(taking off a plastic rain hat and raincoat)
Oh, I wish that rain would let up. It's just plain nasty out there.

KEVIN
(takes off his raincoat and pulls an envelope
out of his breast pocket)
"It's a good day for ducks." Isn't that what Dad used to say?

HAZEL
(ignoring the comment)
Would you like a cup of instant, or do you prefer tea?

KEVIN
Neither, really. I'm stuffed. What did you think of the restaurant?

HAZEL

It seemed rather expensive, Kevin. I mean, $8.00 for a piece of apple crumble? Anyone can make apple crumble.

KEVIN

Maybe. Well, I can't, but I suppose a lot of people can.

HAZEL
(indicating the envelope)
What have you got there?

KEVIN

Just a couple of things that need your signature. Why don't you sit down?

HAZEL

What sort of things? Who would want my signature?

KEVIN

Please, mother, sit down.
(HAZEL sits. KEVIN takes papers out of the envelope.)
Mr. Trout sent these over. First, there's your Living Will. You need to sign at the bottom.
(HAZEL looks vague so he continues.)
Remember? You didn't want any heroic measures at the end.

HAZEL
(signing)
That's true. The question is, will you be able to pull the plug?
Maybe I should have Shirley do it. She's not as tenderhearted.

KEVIN
You didn't mention anything about Shirley.
(He puts another document in front of her.)

HAZEL
There's more?

KEVIN
Yes, this is the POWER OF ATTORNEY … in case you go
crackers and can't manage your affairs.

HAZEL
I manage my affairs quite well, thank you. It's money I have
trouble with. LOL.

KEVIN
LOL?

HAZEL
Where do I sign?

KEVIN
(pointing)

Right here.

HAZEL

I suppose you've got a will in there too?

KEVIN
(putting the papers back into his breast pocket)
You've already got a will, remember?

HAZEL

I knew that.
(Kevin stands and collects his coat.)
You're sure you can't stay for a cup of coffee?

KEVIN

I'm afraid I can't tonight, mother. Jeannie's got ballet at one end of town and Kenny has soccer at the other. You know how it is.
(He kisses her on the cheek.)

HAZEL
(looking at her watch)
Actually, I'm expecting company anyway.

KEVIN
(leaving)
That's wonderful! I'm glad you're making friends here.

HAZEL
Okay, now, run along.

(KEVIN exits.)

KEVIN
(popping his head back in)
By the way, Officer Windham called me. He says you're not returning his phone calls.

HAZEL
(huffy)
I've been too busy. Now, go!
(shuts the door in his face)

(BLACKOUT)

(END OF SCENE)

ACT 1

Scene 5

SETTING: Hazel's room.

AT RISE: HAZEL is bustling around, tidying the room in preparation for HENRY's visit. She's in a bit of a frenzy, checking and rechecking her watch. She finally sits in a chair with an enforced type of calmness. There's a knock at the door. When she opens it she sees HENRY.

HENRY

Hello.
(extending his hand)
You must be Hazel.

HAZEL
(shaking hands with him)

Yes, I am.

HENRY

I'm Henry. I believe you're expecting me.

HAZEL

Yes, Amber said you'd be stopping by. Please, come in.

(As soon as HENRY is through the door HAZEL checks the hallway then closes the door behind him.)

HENRY
(looking around)
This is a nice room. You've got a beautiful view of the garden.

HAZEL
Yes, I quite enjoy it. Please sit down. I could put some tea on.

HENRY
That would be much appreciated.

HAZEL
I prefer decaf this time of night, don't you?

HENRY
Absolutely. Otherwise I'd be up all night.

HAZEL
Cream or sugar?

HENRY
A spot of cream wouldn't go amiss.

HAZEL
(looking over her tea selection in the cupboard)
I've got Orange Pekoe and Earl Grey.

HENRY
I'll leave it up to you. I'm amenable to both.

HAZEL
Earl Grey it is then.

(She pours water from the kettle into the teapot and drops two teabags in. Then she pulls a carton of cream from the bar fridge under the counter and gets the mugs out.)

HENRY
(picking up a picture from
the table in front of him)
Is this your family, Hazel?

HAZEL
Yes. That's my late husband, George, with my son Kevin and his family. It was taken a few years ago.

HENRY
You haven't changed much.

                         HAZEL
That's a kind thing to say.

                         HENRY
What did your husband do?

                         HAZEL
He was a general contractor. Renovations mostly. How about
you?

                         HENRY
                        (laughing)
Me? I was what you'd call a consultant. (Chuckling). That
means I was a Jack-of-all-trades, Master-of-none.

                         HAZEL
                       (concerned)
I see.

                         HENRY
Oh dear, I think I just made myself out as a loser. Let me assure
you, I was quite successful.

                         HAZEL
          (relieved, she pours the tea into the mugs)
The working life seems so far away now, doesn't it? Like it
didn't really happen.

HENRY
(taking his mug)
It does, now that you mention it.
(takes a sip)
Oh, that's good.
(sets down his cup)
What did you do, Hazel? Did you have a life outside the home?

HAZEL
(sitting down across from him with her tea)
Yes, I did. I taught Grade Three for almost forty years.

HENRY
I think you'd have to have nerves of steel to do that.

HAZEL
Do you have children?

HENRY
(shaking his head)
None that I know about. I never married.

HAZEL
That's unusual for a man.

HENRY

I was stupid, you see. I let the girl of my dreams slip through my fingers. I came back from a trip to the Far East and she'd married someone else.

HAZEL

I'm so sorry.

HENRY

Oh, I've taken responsibility for that blunder.

HAZEL

I suppose you filled your life with work after that.

HENRY

That's exactly what I did. And, on balance, it's been a good life. I've been to almost every country in the world and made many friends along the way.

HAZEL

I can't imagine what it would be like to see the world.

HENRY

You haven't travelled?

HAZEL

Not really. George was always busy with his building jobs
during the summer.
(reminiscing)
We did go to Florida one Christmas so that Kevin could see
Disneyworld, but George got very angry at the long lineups. I
never wanted to travel with him after that.

HENRY

That's too bad.

(HENRY's about to take another sip when there's a knock on
the door.)

NURSE

Mrs. Beecham? Are you there? It's the nurse. You forgot to
come down for your medication.

(Flustered, HAZEL whisks the cup out of HENRY's hands,
considers putting it in the sink, then sticks it in the refrigerator.)

HAZEL

JUST A MINUTE! I'LL BE RIGHT THERE!
(grabbing HENRY by the arm and hauling him out of the chair)
You've got to hide!
(HENRY looks stunned.)
In the bathroom! Quick!

(HENRY ducks into the bathroom.)

NURSE

Mrs. Beecham? Are you all right?

HAZEL
(opening the door)

Yes, I'm fine.

NURSE
(looking around the room)

Who were you talking to?

HAZEL

No one. It was just the TV.

(The nurse holds out a tiny cup with her pills.)

NURSE

You're sure you're all right? You look a little flushed.

HAZEL

Fine. It's just a little warm in here.

NURSE

Perhaps if I cracked the window open …

HAZEL
(ushering her out)
I'll do that. Thanks for bringing down my pills. It's been a busy day.

NURSE
Well, you have a good sleep.

(NURSE exits.)
(HAZEL rushes to the bathroom and lets HENRY out.)

HAZEL
Sorry about that. I forgot to go down for my meds.

HENRY
Not a problem. I should be going, anyway.
(walking towards the door)
We could continue our conversation tomorrow night ... if you're not busy.

HAZEL
(flattered)
I'd like that.

HENRY
Good. I'll see you then.

(HAZEL checks the hallway before allowing him to leave.)

(HENRY exits.)

(HAZEL closes the door and leans against it with a satisfied look on her face.)

(BLACKOUT)

(END OF SCENE)

ACT 1

Scene 6

SETTING: Hazel's room.

AT RISE: AMBER hastily closes the bottom dresser drawer as HAZEL enters.

HAZEL
Amber? I almost thought you weren't coming.

AMBER
On the afternoon shift today, Mrs. B. Just finishing up.

HAZEL
Well, I'm expecting Kevin any minute now, so you'd better scoot.

AMBER
You don't think your son would like me?

HAZEL
I know he wouldn't.

AMBER
Why? Have you been telling stories about me?

HAZEL

Just the opposite, Amber. I praise you to the high heavens.

AMBER

And that's a bad thing?

HAZEL

In Kevin's eyes, yes. He's afraid someone will bamboozle him out of his inheritance.

AMBER

Like, you'd put me in your will, Mrs. B?

HAZEL

Something like that.

AMBER

I've never been in a will.

HAZEL

Surely you're in your parents' will?

AMBER
(shaking her head)

My parents are dead, Mrs. B. I thought I told you that. It's just me and my aunt and she doesn't have two nickels to rub together.

HAZEL
(trying to recall something just beyond her grasp)
No, I don't think you mentioned it.
(sees a vase of flowers on the coffee table)
When did these arrive?

AMBER
They were here when I came in. I bet they're from you-know-who. I told you Henry was a top-notch guy.

HAZEL
(thrilled)
They're beautiful.
(delicately fingering the petals)
Pink carnations are my favourite.

AMBER
I'm no expert but I think that means he likes you.

HAZEL
I like him too, but I don't want to rush into anything.

AMBER
(teasing)
Because at your age you can afford to take your time.

HAZEL

Don't be flippant, Amber. Just because I'm old doesn't mean I'm going to throw myself at the first man who comes along.

AMBER
(laughs)
I get it, Mrs. B. You're playing hard to get.

HAZEL

Okay, enough tidying up.

AMBER

Are you seeing him again tonight?

HAZEL

Not that it's any of your business … but, yes.

AMBER
(leaving)
Two words, Mrs. B: Safe Sex.

HAZEL

One word, Amber: Goodbye.

(AMBER exits. HAZEL takes off her sweater, combs her hair, puts on fresh lipstick. There's a knock on the door and KEVIN enters.)

KEVIN

Oh good, you're here.

HAZEL

Where did you think I'd be?

KEVIN

I wasn't sure you'd remember.

HAZEL

I've got Parkinson's, Kevin. Not Alzheimer's.

KEVIN

(Contrite. Sees the flowers and goes over to sniff them.)
These are nice. Are they from the Women's Institute?

HAZEL

That's none ... Well, yes, yes, they are. They must have come
around while I was at lunch. I always miss them.

KEVIN

I wondered if you'd like to go out for a drive? We could take
the lake road and stop at the ice cream parlour.

HAZEL

I'd like that very much. Actually, I've been meaning to ask you ... if I wanted to go out and get my hair done, could I take a taxi over? The hairdresser here just isn't as good as Marie.

KEVIN

It's a retirement home, not a prison, mother. As long as you sign out, you can go wherever you like.

HAZEL

I think I'll do that then.

KEVIN

Shall we be off?

HAZEL

Yes. You've got my mouth watering for a chocolate sundae.

KEVIN
(offering her his arm)
One chocolate sundae coming up!

(BLACKOUT)

(END OF SCENE)

ACT 1

Scene 7

SETTING: Hazel's room.

AT RISE: HENRY and HAZEL enter.

> HAZEL
> (taking off her jacket and hanging it up)
> Well, that was quite an outing!

> HENRY
> It was interesting, Hazel. I haven't been to the symphony in ages.

> HAZEL
> Why don't I put the kettle on? Do you have time for a cup of tea?

> HENRY
> Do you have anything stronger? My back's a bit stiff from all that sitting.

HAZEL

(looks through the cupboard and shakes her head)

Hmm, wait a minute.

(opening the bar fridge)

I've got a bottle of Bailey's from the duty-free shop. Kevin bought it on their way home from Florida.

HENRY

That would be fine. On the rocks, if you don't mind.

HAZEL

I don't mind at all.

(HAZEL pours him his drink and sets it on the coffee table.)

HENRY

Thank you.

(He immediately drains the glass.)

HAZEL

Oh, you *were* thirsty. Would you like another?

HENRY

If it's not too much trouble.

HAZEL

It's no trouble at all.
(pours him another drink then sits down)

HENRY

What made you think of the symphony, Hazel?

HAZEL

It's ironic, really. I was going to cancel my season's tickets and then I thought, why should I? Kevin told me I could go wherever I liked.

HENRY

He sounds like a nice young man.

HAZEL

Yes, he is. He picked out this room. He looked at two others but he knew this was the one.

HENRY
(finishing his glass of Bailey's)

And it was!

HAZEL

I can see everyone coming in from the parking lot. It helps me pass the time.
(eyeing his empty glass)
Would you like another?

HENRY

Please. Bit of sciatica, you know.

HAZEL

Oh, I know how painful that can be.
(pours him another drink then sits down again)
What did you think of the concert? Personally I love it when they do jazz.

HENRY

It was certainly better than something stuffy.

HAZEL

We've got a new conductor, very progressive.

(Henry finishes his drink and stands up.)

HENRY

Well, I'd best be toddling off before I fall asleep in my chair.

HAZEL
(seeing him to the door)
I'm up to planning other outings, if you're interested.

HENRY
(kissing her on the cheek)
That would be wonderful, dear. Do you want to make sure the coast is clear?

HAZEL
(checks the hallway)
It's not you, of course. I'm just not sure of the rules yet. Kevin would have a fit if I got into trouble.

HENRY
(chucking her playfully under the chin)
A little trouble isn't always bad.

HAZEL
(flustered)
Well, good night.

HENRY
Good night, Hazel.

(HAZEL is about to clean up when there's a knock at the door. She opens it to find the NURSE.)

HAZEL

Oh, it's you.

NURSE

Yes, it's me. You forgot to come down for your medication again.

HAZEL

I've just gotten back from the symphony.

NURSE

How nice. I've heard good things about it.
(NURSE hands her the paper cup with her pills in it, then lingers.)
I'm supposed to watch you take them.

HAZEL

(pours herself a glass of water and swallows them)
There you go. Down the hatch.

NURSE

(spotting the bottle of Bailey's)
Have you been drinking, Mrs. Beecham?

HAZEL

Er, just a nightcap.

NURSE

It's best not to mix alcohol with the medication, just as a precaution.

HAZEL
(reluctantly)
I don't usually drink. It was sort of a special occasion.

NURSE

Well, we all need our little celebrations from time to time, don't we? I won't tell if you won't.

(NURSE exits.)

HAZEL
(closing the door behind her)
I wasn't planning to.

(BLACKOUT)

(END OF SCENE)

ACT 1

Scene 8

SETTING: Clinic examination room at the retirement home.

AT RISE: SHIRLEY is being examined by DR. KOMAR.
DR. OLIVER is present.

DR. KOMAR
Would you mind following my finger with your eyes, Miss Townsend?
(Shirley complies as he moves his finger horizontally in front of her face.)
Good.
(steps back)
Have you been feeling any numbness or tingling in your limbs?

SHIRLEY
No.

DR. KOMAR
Headaches? Blurred vision?

SHIRLEY
No.

DR. KOMAR

Slurred speech?

SHIRLEY

Not since it happened, no.

DR. KOMAR

You were one of the lucky ones.

SHIRLEY

It was lucky I was at the supermarket and not home alone. I never fancied being eaten by my dogs.

DR. KOMAR

What did you do with your dogs when you moved here?

SHIRLEY

My sister took one, and I had Roxy, the older one, put to sleep.

DR. KOMAR

That must have been hard.

SHIRLEY

Loss is inevitable at my age, Doctor. Not easy, mind you, but I try to stay positive about things.

DR. KOMAR

They say you live longer if you make plans for the future.
(SHIRLEY chortles)
What's so funny?

SHIRLEY

My friend, Hazel. She lives here, too.

DR. KOMAR

Hazel Beecham? She's a friend of yours?

SHIRLEY

Has been since kindergarten.

DR. KOMAR

What about Hazel made you laugh?

SHIRLEY

She fancies finding a boyfriend before she dies.

DR. KOMAR

A boyfriend?

SHIRLEY
(droll)
Yeah, a guy that takes you out on dates and makes you think
you're his.

DR. KOMAR

You don't think boyfriends are a good idea?

SHIRLEY

I think the only people who want them are the ones who don't
have them.

DR. KOMAR

What about you?

SHIRLEY
(testy)

What about me?

DR. KOMAR

Do you have plans for the future?

SHIRLEY

I used to, before the stroke. I was getting ready to take a cruise
when BAM, my whole life changed. Now I live in a sea of
walkers.

DR. KOMAR

But you made a full recovery. Why did you move here?

SHIRLEY

Because of Hazel. She didn't want to be here and she was very unhappy.

DR. KOMAR

You moved here because of her?

SHIRLEY

Yes. She's my best friend ... and she hasn't had an easy life.
(DR. KOMAR looks at her quizzically.)
She was a little combat soldier, inflicted with all sorts of damage she couldn't do anything about.

DR. KOMAR

What kind of damage?

SHIRLEY

Her husband, George, was a brute when he was in the sauce.

DR. KOMAR

I wasn't aware of that.

SHIRLEY

No, you wouldn't be. She locked up her past years ago and threw away the key.

DR. KOMAR

But you say she wants a boyfriend? Wouldn't that be the last
thing she'd want?

SHIRLEY
(shrugs)

You'd think so, wouldn't you?
(looking at her watch, then slipping off the examining table)
Well, I'm going to be late for my euchre game, so if there's
nothing else …

DR. OLIVER
(slowing her down)

Miss Townsend, if you happen to notice that Mrs. Beecham
seems, well, not quite right, would you please inform the duty
nurse?

SHIRLEY
(tossing her head back laughing as she leaves)

Hazel, not quite right? That's rich!

(SHIRLEY exits.)

DR. KOMAR

That's quite remarkable, isn't it? That Miss Townsend would
give up a normal life to live here with her friend.

DR. OLIVER

We see it quite often amongst spouses. Several of them don't
need to be here.

DR. KOMAR

That's love, I guess.

DR. OLIVER

Of the highest order, if you ask me.

(Knock at the door. NURSE pops her head in.)

NURSE

Mrs. Beecham is here for her appointment.

(She falls back and HAZEL enters.)

DR. OLIVER

Mrs. Beecham? How are you today?

HAZEL

Fine, thank you. (Looking at DR. KOMAR.) Oh, hello again.

(DR. OLIVER defers to DR. KOMAR.)

DR. KOMAR

Nice to see you again, Hazel. Why don't you take a seat?

HAZEL
(sits down on the examining table)
Thank you.

DR. KOMAR
(referring to her chart)
How have you been feeling, overall?

HAZEL
(happily)
Pretty good.

DR. KOMAR

No tremors?

HAZEL

None at all. The MagnaDopa seems to be doing the trick.

DR. KOMAR

The last time you were in you mentioned seeing coloured triangles as you were falling asleep. Are you still seeing them?

HAZEL

No.

DR. KOMAR
(scribbling on her chart)
Good.

HAZEL
I see faces instead.

(Both doctors are suddenly attentive.)

DR. KOMAR
Pardon?

HAZEL
I see faces - faces of people I've never seen before. They flash
on the inside of my eyelids like a slide show. Some of them are
quite odd-looking.

DR. OLIVER
(interjecting)
Does this happen every night?

HAZEL
No, not every night.

DR. OLIVER
Have you seen them during the day?

HAZEL

No.

DR. OLIVER

Do you see other unusual things?

HAZEL

Like what?

DR. OLIVER

Things that are out of place. Like, an elephant in the dining room, for instance.

HAZEL
(laughing)

An elephant in the dining room? That would really liven things up!
(looking at the doctors' concerned faces)
What? Am I losing my mind?

DR. OLIVER
(reassuringly)

Nothing of the sort, Mrs. Beecham, but the drug manufacturer may want to pull you out of the trial.

HAZEL
(upset)
You mean, no more MagnaDopa? I'd start shaking again?
I don't want to hear that.

DR. OLIVER
There's no reason to worry. As soon as the drug's out of your
system we'll start you on something else.

HAZEL
But what if it doesn't work?

DR. OLIVER
(helping her off the table)
We'll do our best to minimize any symptoms you may have,
Mrs. Beecham.

HAZEL
(shaking her head)
Oh dear. I hope this doesn't ruin everything.

(HAZEL exits.)

DR. KOMAR
I think I understand why she's so upset. Remember, Miss
Townsend said she wanted a boyfriend? I bet she's found one.

DR. OLIVER

Stranger things have happened.

(BLACKOUT)

(END OF SCENE)

ACT 1

Scene 9

SETTING: A patio outside the Peach Gardens Retirement Home.

AT RISE: HAZEL and SHIRLEY are having coffee.

> HAZEL
> (lowering the cup from her lips)

It was a wonderful idea, having our coffee out here. It's a beautiful day.

> SHIRLEY
> (breathing deeply)

Don't you just want to savour every moment like this?

> HAZEL

Shirley, the only reason I'm getting by in this place is because you're here.

> SHIRLEY
> (reaching over and taking her hand)

We have a pact, remember? BOSOM BUDDIES FOREVER!

HAZEL
(matter-of-factly)
They're called racks now.

SHIRLEY
What's called racks?

HAZEL
Bosoms.

SHIRLEY
Who told you that?

HAZEL
Amber.

SHIRLEY
(frowning)
Makes me feel like I'm in the wrong century.

HAZEL
Me too.

SHIRLEY
That guy she set you up with, how's that working out?

                    HAZEL
Very well, actually. It's surprising.

                    SHIRLEY
                    (teasing)
So ... what's his name?

                    HAZEL
                    (shyly)
Henry.

                    SHIRLEY
I don't think I know any Henrys. Where's he from?

                    HAZEL
I ... I'm not sure. It hasn't come up.

                    SHIRLEY
Is he good-looking?

                    HAZEL
Very. And he's been everywhere. He had to travel the world for
his job.

                    SHIRLEY
It's been so long since I've had a date, I don't think I'd know
what to do.

HAZEL

Mostly we just talk. I know it doesn't sound like much, but he's easy to talk to.

(NURSE approaches their table.)

NURSE

Sorry to interrupt, ladies.

SHIRLEY
(surprised)
Did one of us miss an appointment?

NURSE

No, you're both fine. I'm just taking a survey to see if anyone's missing any jewellery.

SHIRLEY

Jewellery? Why?

NURSE

Some of the residents have reported items being stolen.
(HAZEL looks a bit stunned.)
Mrs. Beecham?

HAZEL
(shaking her head)
I don't think so but I'll doublecheck.

NURSE
Please do that and let me know. You too, Miss Townsend.

SHIRLEY
Sure.

(NURSE exits.)

What was that all about? You disappeared into your head for a second.

HAZEL
I was thinking about Amber.

SHIRLEY
(taking another sip of coffee)
Amber? Why?

HAZEL
(looking around to make sure no one can hear)
Because, Amber's a thief.

                    SHIRLEY
                  (taken aback)
What?

                    HAZEL
She is.

                    SHIRLEY
That can't be right. They wouldn't let a thief work here.

                    HAZEL
Amber's not an employee. She's doing community service to
work off a sentence. If she puts in so many hours, she doesn't
have to go to jail.

                    SHIRLEY
                (raising an eyebrow)
How extraordinary. What did she steal?

                    HAZEL
A watch, apparently.

                    SHIRLEY
Just one?

HAZEL

So she says. She was caught leaving a store with it and they pressed charges. Oh, I hope it's not her. She's been so good to me.

SHIRLEY

Did she say *why* she stole the watch?

HAZEL

She couldn't give a reason other than it was a bad point in her life.

SHIRLEY

That's it? A bad point in her life and it's okay to steal?

HAZEL

She didn't say it was okay.

SHIRLEY

It's an excuse, isn't it? Rough time at home, knock over a little old lady and steal her purse.

HAZEL

She didn't do that!

SHIRLEY

I was speaking metaphorically.

HAZEL

Well, stop it. Amber's a perfectly nice girl.

SHIRLEY

Then why are you worried she might be stealing people's jewellery?

HAZEL
(annoyed)
I don't know. I guess I'm not really.

SHIRLEY

I'd talk to her about it, if I were you.

HAZEL

You mean, come right out and ask her?

SHIRLEY
(looking over her cup at HAZEL)
That's exactly what I mean. Get to the bottom of it. Save us little old ladies the aggravation of trying to remember where we put our pearl earrings.

HAZEL

Well, I … I don't know if I could do that.

SHIRLEY

It can't hurt, can it?
(HAZEL is thinking about this when there's a rumble of
thunder. They both look up at the sky.)
It's easy to let things slide, pretend they're not happening.
You've been guilty of that in the past.

HAZEL

I don't like confrontation, Shirley. I'm not good at it.

SHIRLEY

Maybe it would help her.

HAZEL

I'm not a therapist!

SHIRLEY

I know, but talking it out might help you both.

HAZEL

How would it help me?

SHIRLEY

Well, isn't it logical that once you start confronting things, it
gets easier?
(There's another rumble of thunder.)
It looks like the weather's turned. We'd better get inside.

(They quickly grab their cups and exit.)

(CURTAIN)

(END OF ACT)

ACT 2

Scene 1

SETTING: Hazel's room.

AT RISE: SHIRLEY arrives to walk HAZEL down for dinner.

SHIRLEY

Are you ready?

(HAZEL is pacing, wringing her hands, clearly agitated.)

What is it? What's the matter?

HAZEL

Close the door!

(SHIRLEY closes the door.)

SHIRLEY
(grabs hold of HAZEL to keep her from pacing)
Okay, calm down. You know Dr. Oliver doesn't like it when you get like this.

HAZEL
(hissing)

It's happened to me!

SHIRLEY

What's happened to you?

HAZEL

My pin! It's gone!

SHIRLEY

What pin?

HAZEL

The diamond and emerald pin that belonged to my mother.

SHIRLEY

When did you lose it?

HAZEL

I didn't lose it! It was right here in my jewellery box, where I
always keep it!

SHIRLEY

Why don't I take a look? Maybe you couldn't see it for
looking. It happens to me all the time.

HAZEL
(takes the jewellery box from the dresser and
places it on the table)
Fine!

(SHIRLEY sits down and opens it. She moves things around on
the first row and then moves to the bottom row.)

SHIRLEY
I don't see it here.

HAZEL
(victorious)
I told you it wasn't there. It's gone, just like everyone else's!

SHIRLEY
Let's not jump to conclusions, Hazel.
(puts the jewellery box back on the dresser)
It could have slipped into the drawer, couldn't it?

HAZEL
Fine, Miss Marple. Take a look.

SHIRLEY

(opening the drawer)

Your dainties are so neat. Mine are in such a jumble.

(carries on a careful search)

I don't see it here. Do you mind if I look in the other drawers?

HAZEL

Go ahead. I just want it back. It's my best piece.

(SHIRLEY finds nothing in the second drawer and proceeds to search the bottom one. Suddenly her hand emerges holding the brooch.)

SHIRLEY

Is this it?

HAZEL

(taking it from her and pressing it to her chest)

Oh, thank goodness! You found it!

(plunks herself into a chair)

I'd almost lost faith, Shirley. I was in such a moral dilemma. But it wasn't Amber. She didn't steal it!

SHIRLEY

(lifting out a handful of jewellery from the drawer)

Then, how do you explain this?

HAZEL
(getting worked up again)
What? No! It can't be! It can't!

SHIRLEY
I'm afraid it is.

HAZEL
Please Shirley, don't tell anyone. She just needs a chance in life. Haven't we all needed a chance at one time or another?

SHIRLEY
Hazel, I have no choice but to report it.

HAZEL
But she'll lose her job! She might go to jail! Have some compassion, Shirley! You've got to!

SHIRLEY
(putting a hand on HAZEL's sleeve to console her)
Okay, I promise I won't mention Amber's name.

HAZEL
Cross your throat and hope to choke?

SHIRLEY

Cross my throat and hope to choke. Now, if we don't get down
to dinner we'll be warming up a can of beans in the
microwave.

(HAZEL smiles and puts her arm through SHIRLEY's as they
exit.)

(BLACKOUT)

(END OF SCENE)

ACT 2

Scene 2

SETTING: Hazel's room.

AT RISE: KEVIN is consoling HAZEL.

KEVIN
Mother, please stop crying and tell me what's the matter.

HAZEL
(shaking her head, crying despondently into a handkerchief)
How would that help? There's nothing you can do.

KEVIN
How do you know? Why don't we talk about it?

HAZEL
(sitting down)
All right. You know the girl who cleans my room? Amber?

KEVIN
Not personally, but go on.

HAZEL

Well, there's a problem with her. A serious problem.

KEVIN
(anxious)

No one told me about any problem.

HAZEL

I'm not going to tell you if you're going to fly off the handle.

KEVIN

All right, go on.

HAZEL

She's been stealing. Oh, don't act so surprised, Kevin. I'm sure it happens all the time in places like this.

KEVIN

But mother, this place costs a fortune! The staff must need police clearances to work here!

HAZEL

Amber isn't one of the regular staff. She got into some trouble with the law and she's doing community service.

KEVIN

What? That's so fantastical I can hardly believe it.

HAZEL

Which part?

KEVIN

The fact that the Peach Gardens Retirement Home would allow such a thing.

HAZEL

Maybe they have no choice. Those people have to go somewhere, don't they?

KEVIN

Not to a retirement home full of vulnerable people, they don't. What's she stealing?

HAZEL

Jewellery.

KEVIN
(agitated)
Well, I'm going to have to speak to someone about this!

HAZEL
(crying)
You can't, Kevin! You said you wouldn't fly off the handle!

KEVIN

You're right. Continue.

HAZEL

Some of the residents started missing things … watches, bracelets, that sort of thing. Then, one day, my brooch was gone. Shirley thought I'd just mislaid it so she looked through my dresser drawers. And that's when she found the jewellery.

KEVIN
(his voice flattens at this development)

Oh.

HAZEL

Yes, oh.

KEVIN
(burying his head in his hands)

Where is it now?

HAZEL

Shirley took it. She promised not to mention Amber when she turns it in. If they find out, her life will be ruined.

KEVIN

I understand.

HAZEL
(edgy)
Amber's very important to me, almost a friend. You're always
saying I could use more of those.

KEVIN
What do you want me to do?

HAZEL
Just find out what happened. Discreetly.

KEVIN
All right, I'll try.
(kisses HAZEL on top of her head then switches on the TV as
he's leaving)
There you go. Jeopardy's on.

HAZEL
(suddenly springing to life)
Jeopardy! That means it's past 7:30!

KEVIN
So it is.

HAZEL
(shoving Kevin out the door)
Well, thank you for your visit.

KEVIN
(puzzled)

What?

HAZEL

You'll be home just in time to tuck the kiddies in. Goodbye.

(KEVIN exits.)

(HAZEL, humming, starts tidying up the room)

(BLACKOUT)

(END OF SCENE)

Act 2

Scene 3

SETTING: Hazel's room.

AT RISE: HENRY and HAZEL enter. HAZEL carries a wet umbrella.)

HENRY
I've never seen a colder, wetter rain.

HAZEL
(heading for the bathroom with the umbrella)
As soon as I dump this in the tub I'll put the tea on so we don't catch our death of cold.

HENRY
You wouldn't happen to have something a wee bit stronger, would you?

HAZEL
(comes out from the bathroom and heads for the fridge)
There's just the Bailey's, I'm afraid, until Kevin goes on another vacation.

HENRY

That will do.

(Hazel pours his drink and puts the kettle on for herself. Then she sits down across from Henry.)

HAZEL

I'm sorry about the movie. I didn't know it was going to be a chick flick. I could tell by the way you were fidgeting that you would have preferred an action movie.

HENRY

I won't deny it. I prefer a lot of shooting and a car chase.

HAZEL

Who was the fellow that played Diane Keaton's husband?

HENRY

Morgan Freeman?

HAZEL

Yes! What else have I seen him in?

HENRY
(looks at her peculiarly)

How would I know?

HAZEL
(racking her brain)
Oh, I know … it was that funny movie with … oh, what's his name … the Canadian guy … made it big in Hollywood … it's on the tip of my tongue.

HENRY
Martin Short?

HAZEL
No, no, taller than that. He has an elastic face.

HENRY
Elastic face?

HAZEL
You know, he keeps turning green and has a funny little dog?

HENRY
Jim Carrey?

HAZEL
That's it! Jim Carrey! What was the name of that film? It was so funny.

HENRY

I don't have a clue. How did we get onto Jim Carrey? He wasn't in the film.

HAZEL

(trying to think back to the beginning of the conversation)
I forget. Anyway, he's terribly handsome, isn't he?

HENRY

Who? Morgan Freeman or Jim Carrey?

HAZEL

That's it! Morgan Freeman! He was God and he gave the job over to Jim Carrey!

HENRY

I'm glad we got that cleared up.
(HAZEL hears the kettle and gets up to make her cup of tea.)
Do you like your men tall and lean, Hazel?

HAZEL

Men? I've only had one man.

HENRY

How about balding and a little paunchy?

HAZEL
(laughs self-consciously)
I guess I must. Would you like anything to go with your drink?

HENRY
No, this is fine. The popcorn really filled me up.

HAZEL
I think I'll have a couple of biscuits.

HENRY
Suit yourself.
(hands HAZEL his empty glass)
Is there enough for a top up?

HAZEL
(frowning)
A little, I think.
(HAZEL gets a couple of cookies from a bag and puts them on a plate then pours HENRY another drink. She hands it to him then sits down.)
I'm afraid that's the last of it.

HENRY
I guess we'll have to stop at the Liquor Store the next time we're out.

HAZEL
(annoyed)
Why? Is it really that important to you?

HENRY
What?

HAZEL
The booze?

HENRY
I don't see anything wrong with it after a wonderful evening.

HAZEL
But, is it every evening? Is it a regular thing?

HENRY
With moderation. It's nothing I can't handle.

HAZEL
How do you know you can handle it?

HENRY
(getting to his feet)
I think I can see where this conversation is headed.

HAZEL

It was a simple question.

HENRY

A question for another time.

HAZEL

You're going? Just because I asked you about your drinking?

HENRY

It's late and I don't have the head for this right now.
(opens the door)
Thank you for a nice evening.

HAZEL

But ...

(HENRY exits.)

(BLACKOUT)

(END OF SCENE)

Act 2

Scene 4

SETTING: Outside the door of the clinic at the Peach Gardens Retirement Home.

AT RISE: KEVIN arrives at the clinic just as SHIRLEY is leaving.

> SHIRLEY
> (surprised)
> Kevin! I didn't expect to see you here.

> KEVIN
> I've been summoned.

> SHIRLEY
> About Hazel?

> KEVIN
> They're thinking about taking her off the MagnaDopa.

> SHIRLEY
> But why? She's been doing so well.

KEVIN

Apparently, there's a problem of some sort.

SHIRLEY

Oh?

KEVIN

She *has* been acting a little peculiar lately. A friend of mine said he saw her at the symphony the other night! Can you imagine?

SHIRLEY

Well, why shouldn't she go? She's got season's tickets.

KEVIN

(snorting derisively)

I know, but I didn't expect her to use them! And then there's this business with the jewellery. She said that you turned it in.

SHIRLEY

I had to, Kevin.

KEVIN

I'm not blaming you. I'm just wondering what you said when you dropped it off.

SHIRLEY

I said I found it stashed in the laundry room.

KEVIN
(relieved)
That's brilliant! She was so afraid Amber was going to lose her job.

SHIRLEY

No worries there, Kevin. No one's going to lose their job.

(DR. OLIVER opens the door.)

DR. OLIVER

Mr. Beecham? Would you like to come in?

KEVIN

Right.

SHIRLEY

We'll talk again sometime.

(SHIRLEY exits.)

(KEVIN enters the room.)

(DR. OLIVER and DR. KOMAR are present.)

DR. OLIVER

Would you like to take a seat?

KEVIN

No, I'll stand, if you don't mind.

DR. OLIVER
(flipping open his mother's chart)
Very well. Just to go over a bit of history here: your mother
was diagnosed with Parkinson's Disease in May of this year.
The predominant symptom was shakiness in her hands.

KEVIN

That's right.

DR. OLIVER

Since then she's been taking part in the clinical trial of a new
drug called MagnaDopa.

KEVIN

Yes. It seems to have improved her condition quite a bit.

DR. OLIVER

We've made the same observation, Mr. Beecham.
Unfortunately, she's been exhibiting some side effects ... not
serious side effects, but the drug manufacturer doesn't want to
take any chances.

KEVIN

What sort of side effects?

DR. OLIVER

She's seeing geometric patterns or faces before she drifts off to sleep. They're mild hallucinations, not unusual, or dangerous, but MagnaDopa is still in the trial stage and the drug company wants us to take her off it.

KEVIN

So, what happens now?

DR. OLIVER

As soon as we're sure it's out of her system we'll start her on another drug.

KEVIN

What about the shaking?

DR. OLIVER

To be honest, coming off the MagnaDopa will be rough - and you might notice some mood swings. But once she's on the new medication, everything will be fine.

KEVIN

But, what if she has the same side effects on the new drug?

DR. OLIVER

As I said, it's not something we'd normally concern ourselves with.

KEVIN

Are you going to let her know, or should I?

DR. OLIVER

We'll tell her. We just wanted you to be aware of what was happening. She's going to need your reassurance and understanding during the transition period.

KEVIN
(leaving, slightly bewildered)
Well, thanks for letting me know.

DR. OLIVER

No trouble at all, Mr. Beecham.

(BLACKOUT)

(END OF SCENE)

Act 2

Scene 5

SETTING: Hazel's room. Dark.

AT RISE: SHIRLEY pokes her head into the darkness.

                        SHIRLEY
Hazel? Are you in there?

                        HAZEL
                    (quietly, from her bed)
I'm here.

(Shirley turns on the light.)

                        SHIRLEY
What are you doing? Why aren't you ready for breakfast?

                        HAZEL
                    (sniffling)
I'm not going down.

                        SHIRLEY
Why not? Are you ill?

                    HAZEL
                   (sobbing)
My heart ...

                    SHIRLEY
                   (alarmed)
Your heart! Did you pull the bedside alarm?

                    HAZEL
               (waving her away)
My heart is broken.

                    SHIRLEY
Oh. I guess the paramedics can't help you with that.

                    HAZEL
               (sitting up in bed)
No.

                    SHIRLEY
Is it Henry? Or something else?

                    HAZEL
It's Henry.

(HAZEL gets out of bed.)

SHIRLEY

What did he do?

HAZEL
(agitated, crying)
Henry didn't do anything! I did! I managed to wreck it all by myself.

SHIRLEY

Try to calm down, honey.

HAZEL
(fluttering around the room, gesticulating)
How can I calm down? I blew it, Shirley! I blew it!

SHIRLEY

You're going to have to give me more to go on, Hazel.

HAZEL

We had a fight. A big blow-up. He's a lush, Shirley! I didn't see it in the beginning. It was just some Bailey's when he came over. Then it was all the time.

SHIRLEY
(hopeful)
And you confronted him about it?

HAZEL

I should have kept my mouth shut. But no! I had to make a big deal of it! What was I thinking?

SHIRLEY

For something like that, I think you're justified.

HAZEL

But he didn't want to talk about it! He got mad, said I was meddling and that it wasn't any of my business.

SHIRLEY

But what good would it do to pretend it's not happening? Isn't it better to confront it?

HAZEL
(turning on her)
No, can't you see? That's the wrong advice! Why did I do it, Shirley? Why? Nobody's perfect.

SHIRLEY

You've used that reasoning before, and we both know how that turned out. Maybe you should look at this experience another way. You've finally broken through the silence. After forty years of having your life repeatedly thrown into turmoil by George, you've SAID something! That's a victory!

HAZEL

A victory? I'm a fool. I had a good thing going and now I've got nothing!

SHIRLEY

Look, why don't you tell Henry about your life with George? Maybe if he knew what you went through he'd understand why his drinking bothers you so much.

HAZEL

How can I do that when I've run him off?

SHIRLEY

Hazel, I've run off a lot of men in my lifetime and one thing I can tell you is, they always come back.

HAZEL
(quietly)

I think Henry's too proud.

SHIRLEY

Well, if he doesn't come around, all I can say is "goodbye to bad rubbish".
(softly)

Look, Hazel, I'm sorry he's gone.

HAZEL

I know.

SHIRLEY

Do you want me to bring you something from the dining room?

HAZEL

Toast would be nice.

SHIRLEY

Why don't you get yourself fixed up?

HAZEL
(dejectedly)

What would be the point?

(SHIRLEY nods sadly to her as she exits.
HAZEL crawls back into bed and pulls the covers up.
Moments later there's a knock at the door and
SALLY enters carrying a bouquet of flowers.)

SALLY

Mrs. Beecham? It's Sally from the Women's Institute. Is everything all right?

HAZEL

I don't want to see anyone today. Please go away.

(HAZEL picks up a glass of water but her hand trembles so violently that it slops all over and she puts it down.)

                         SALLY
              (lifts the vase of flowers off the coffee table)
I'll just replace your flowers and be off.

                         HAZEL
              (screams from her bed)
YOU LEAVE THOSE FLOWERS ALONE!

                         SALLY
But Mrs. Beecham, they're all wilted.

                         HAZEL
GET OUT! DO YOU HEAR ME! GET OUT OF HERE!

(SALLY exits,cringing.)

(BLACKOUT)

(END OF SCENE)

ACT 2

Scene 5

SETTING: Hazel's room.

AT RISE: HAZEL is still in bed. A plate is on a tray by her bed. There's a knock at the door and KEVIN enters.

KEVIN

Mother? Are you awake?

HAZEL
(feebly)
Yes. What are you doing here?

KEVIN

Shirley called me. She was concerned.

(goes to her bedside)

HAZEL

She shouldn't have done that. There's nothing you can do.

KEVIN

Do you want to tell me what's the matter?

HAZEL
(shaking her head)

Not particularly.

KEVIN
(sighs as he sits down on the edge of the bed)
The doctor said this might happen.

HAZEL

What? That I'd have my heart broken? He must be psychic.

KEVIN
(puzzled)
You've had your heart broken? By whom?

HAZEL

You said Shirley talked to you.

KEVIN

She said you needed cheering up. I assumed it was because
you're coming off the MagnaDopa.

HAZEL

I am! I'm shaking like a leaf!

KEVIN

But you said your heart's broken.

                            HAZEL

That's a separate issue.

                            KEVIN

So, tell me.

                            HAZEL
                (looking at him tentatively)
I started seeing someone.

                            KEVIN
                        (surprised)
Seeing someone? As in, dating?

                            HAZEL

Yes. What's so shocking about that?

                            KEVIN

Nothing. Nothing at all.

                            HAZEL

Actually, it's the fellow I went to the symphony with. His
name's Henry.

                            KEVIN

And, what do you do with this Henry?

HAZEL

Mainly we talk, but a couple of times we've gone out - once to
the symphony, as you know, and once to the movies.
(KEVIN's eyebrows arch.)
What? You said I could go wherever I liked.

KEVIN

I didn't mean gallivanting all over town!

HAZEL
(annoyed)
Don't treat me like a child, Kevin. You said I wasn't a prisoner
here, that I could take a taxi!

KEVIN

I meant to the hairdresser's, mother.

HAZEL

Fine. You're so smart, I'm not going to tell you the rest.

KEVIN
(picking up the tray)
Suit yourself. I'll run this back to the kitchen. Is there anything
you need before I go?

HAZEL

What about Amber? She wasn't here today. Did she lose her
job?

KEVIN

Maybe she took a sick day. Look mother, I've really got to get
back to work.

HAZEL
(waving him off)

Fine. Go.

(KEVIN exits.)

(BLACKOUT)

(END OF SCENE)

ACT 2

Scene 6

SETTING: Police Interrogation Room.

AT RISE: OFFICER WINDHAM, KEVIN, AND HAZEL are seated around a table. HAZEL locks her hands together to keep them from shaking.

OFFICER WINDHAM
Mrs. Beecham, Mr. Beecham, thank you for coming in.

HAZEL
I don't know why I had to come in again. You don't seem to be doing anything.

KEVIN
(tersely)
Mother, let Officer Windham talk.

HAZEL
What is there to talk about? A man tried to swindle me out of my life savings and stuck a gun in my ribs and *I'm* the one being hauled in here for a dressing down!

OFFICER WINDHAM

I can assure you, Mrs. Beecham, this is nothing of the sort. In fact, I have some good news for you. The case is going to trial next month.

KEVIN

That's great! Isn't it, mother?

HAZEL

Miraculous, I would say.

OFFICER WINDHAM

Naturally the Crown will be calling you as a witness, Mrs. Beecham.

HAZEL

I should hope so!

OFFICER WINDHAM

In order to present you as a credible witness, there's just one thing we need to clear up.

HAZEL
(offended)

A *credible* witness?

OFFICER WINDHAM

Yes. Cases of this nature often turn out to be a "he said/ she said" affair. It'll be a question of who the jury believes.

KEVIN

Even with scores of witnesses?

OFFICER WINDHAM

The defendant's name is Victor Branch. His lawyer will likely argue that Mr. Branch was simply standing in line to carry out a bank transaction when your mother went berserk, causing him to flee.

HAZEL

With a gun pointed at me? What about that?

OFFICER WINDHAM

Well, the gun's a problem. We haven't located it yet.

KEVIN

He could have thrown it into a passing vehicle or passed it to an accomplice, couldn't he?

OFFICER WINDHAM

Perhaps. But nothing like that has come to light.

                              KEVIN
But he has a record!

                        OFFICER WINDHAM
Yes ... but so does your mother.

(KEVIN gasps)

Which is why I've asked you in here.

(HAZEL hangs her head sheepishly.)

                              KEVIN
Mother?

                        OFFICER WINDHAM
It's a juvenile record and I can't force you to tell me about it,
Mrs. Beecham, but defence counsel can bring it up to taint the
credibility of your testimony.

                              HAZEL
                           (indignantly)
In other words, I'll be the one on trial.

                        OFFICER WINDHAM
All I'm saying is that it would help the prosecution if you
explain what happened.

HAZEL
(rising to her feet)
WELL THEN, FORGET THE WHOLE THING! LET HIM
GET OFF SCOTT FREE SO THAT HE CAN TERRORIZE
OTHER LITTLE OLD LADIES!

OFFICER WINDHAM
The charges were brought by the Crown, Mrs. Beecham, so the
trial will proceed regardless. It's not going to be forgotten.

KEVIN
Mother, listen to me. You had a rough life after your parents
died. Nobody's going to blame you for mistakes you made
then.

OFFICER WINDHAM
That's absolutely correct, Mrs. Beecham.

HAZEL
(vigorously shaking her head)
No! I'm not going to do it!

OFFICER WINDHAM
I'm sorry to hear that. It's unfortunate, but it's your choice.

HAZEL
I'd like to go now.

OFFICER WINDHAM

Very well.

(OFFICER WINDHAM starts packing up.
KEVIN motions him to hold up.)

KEVIN

Mother, would you wait for me in the car while I have a word
with Officer Windham?

HAZEL
(tersely)

Fine.

(HAZEL exits.)

KEVIN

Look, I don't know what's in this juvenile file but I can take an
educated guess.

OFFICER WINDHAM

Oh?

KEVIN

My mother is a bit of a kleptomaniac. She picks up things without being aware of it. Maybe she got into some trouble over it when she was young.

OFFICER WINDHAM

I see.

KEVIN

Her parents were killed in a car accident and she had it pretty rough afterwards.

OFFICER WINDHAM

Do you think you can convince her to talk to us?

KEVIN

The way things are right now, Officer, I'd rather not push it.

OFFICER WINDHAM

Mr. Beecham, rest assured, the prosecution will do its best, regardless.

KEVIN

But this Victor Branch might walk?

OFFICER WINDHAM

Yes, he might.

                    KEVIN
That would be a shame.

                OFFICER WINDHAM
Yes, it would.

(BLACKOUT)

(END OF SCENE)

ACT 2

Scene 7

SETTING: Patio at the Peach Gardens Retirement Home.

AT RISE: SHIRLEY is sitting at one of the patio tables enjoying a cup of coffee when HAZEL bursts in on her.

HAZEL
(menacingly)

There you are!

SHIRLEY
(looking up in surprise)

There *you* are! Where have you been?

HAZEL

You did it, didn't you?

SHIRLEY

Did what?

HAZEL

You told on her, didn't you, you traitor!

SHIRLEY

Told on who? Are you talking about Amber?

HAZEL

Of course I'm talking about Amber! What other innocent
people have you betrayed?

SHIRLEY

Keep your voice down, Hazel. Let me get you a cup of coffee.

HAZEL

I'm not interested in having coffee with you.

SHIRLEY

No, let's talk this out. I don't want you to think badly of me
when I didn't do anything.

HAZEL

I'm afraid that would be impossible! The proof is in the
pudding!

SHIRLEY

I don't know what you're talking about.

HAZEL

Don't know what I'm talking about? She's gone, Shirley, gone.
What do you have to say about that?

SHIRLEY
(looking around)
Would you please lower your voice? People are starting to
stare.

HAZEL
What was it, Shirley? Jealousy? Were you afraid Amber was
getting too close? Afraid you'd lose your status as my best
friend?

SHIRLEY
Hazel, for heaven's sake!

HAZEL
Well, you can consider it lost, Shirley. I trusted you and you let
me down in the worst possible way.

SHIRLEY
Amber did not lose her job.

HAZEL
(cooling a bit)
You mean, you've seen her?

SHIRLEY
No, I haven't seen her, but I know she didn't lose her job.

HAZEL

How can you be so sure if you haven't seen her?

(NURSE enters)

NURSE

Is everything all right here? The shouting is making the other residents nervous.

HAZEL
(addressing NURSE)

Maybe *you* can tell me what happened to Amber. Has she lost her job, or not?

NURSE

Amber? I don't think I know her.

SHIRLEY
(getting up hastily from the
table and taking HAZEL's arm)

Perhaps Amber is working in another section, Hazel. Why don't we take a look?

HAZEL
(wriggling out of Shirley's grip)

Don't touch me, you Judas! Stay away from me! I never want to see you again!

(HAZEL exits.)
(SHIRLEY stands there in shock.)

NURSE

She just hasn't been herself lately, has she? Coming off the MagnaDopa, I suppose. It's affecting everyone differently.

SHIRLEY
(looking hard at her)
What do you mean, everyone?

NURSE

Everyone who was on the drug.

SHIRLEY

You mean, they took everybody off it?

NURSE

Yes. There was an unexpected side effect and they had to cancel the trial.

SHIRLEY

What was the side effect?

NURSE

Hallucinations, apparently.

SHIRLEY

So, they know.

NURSE

Know what, Miss Townsend?

SHIRLEY
(shaking her head)
Never mind. It doesn't matter.

(BLACKOUT)

(END OF SCENE)

ACT 2

Scene 8

SETTING: The clinic at the Peach Gardens Retirement Home.

AT RISE: DR. OLIVER and DR. KOMAR are conferring over a patient's chart.

(There's a knock at the door.)

                    DR. OLIVER
Did we miss someone? I thought we were finished.

                    DR. KOMAR
                (opening the door)
Miss Townsend. This is unexpected. Please come in.

                    SHIRLEY
Thank you.

                    DR. KOMAR
What can we do for you?

                    SHIRLEY
Actually, I'm not here about me. It's about my friend, Hazel
Beecham.

DR. KOMAR
(indicating a chair)
Please, sit down.
(SHIRLEY sits)
Is something wrong with Hazel?

SHIRLEY
You could say that. She's been having problems ever since you took her off the MagnaDopa.

DR. KOMAR
You mean the shaking? That's only temporary until she starts her new medication.

SHIRLEY
No, it's not that. She had a side effect from the MagnaDopa.

DR. KOMAR
Yes, we know. That's why the trial was cancelled.

SHIRLEY
I think you should make an exception in Hazel's case.

DR. KOMAR
An exception? Why?

                    SHIRLEY

Because Hazel's hallucinations were good hallucinations.

                   DR. KOMAR

Good hallucinations?

                    SHIRLEY

Yes. They brought her happiness. Now they're gone and she's
miserable.

                   DR. OLIVER
                  (interjecting)

Miss Townsend, Mrs. Beecham's hallucinations were very
minor. She was seeing patterns and faces as she drifted off to
sleep. I can't see how the absence of them would cause her any
distress.

                    SHIRLEY

Patterns? Faces? What are you talking about?

                   DR. KOMAR
               (interrupting gently)

What are *you* talking about, Miss Townsend?

                    SHIRLEY

I'm talking about Amber and Henry.

DR. KOMAR

Who are Amber and Henry?

SHIRLEY

Henry is her boyfriend - or was, anyway - and Amber is the girl
who cleans her room.

DR. OLIVER

And you think Mrs. Beecham has been hallucinating them?

SHIRLEY

Yes. I know all the cleaners here.

DR. OLIVER

And the boyfriend? How do you know he's not real?

SHIRLEY

Because Amber introduced him to her.

DR. KOMAR

And one hallucination could only be introduced by another
hallucination.

SHIRLEY

Exactly.

DR. OLIVER

There *were* reports of fully-developed hallucinations on the drug, but I assure you we had no idea Mrs. Beecham was experiencing them.

DR. KOMAR

But you said Amber and Henry are gone.

SHIRLEY

Yes. They disappeared as soon as you took Hazel off the MagnaDopa. Hazel thinks they've left for other reasons - and she blames me.

DR. OLIVER

I'm sorry about that, but I don't see how we can help.

SHIRLEY

You've got to put her back on it! If you don't, I'm going to lose my best friend.

DR. OLIVER

Miss Townsend, professional ethics prevent us from doing such a thing.

SHIRLEY

Even though the drug gave her a little bit of happiness? Under
the circumstances, I'd say it was spectacularly successful!

DR. KOMAR

It's extraordinary, really.

SHIRLEY

What's extraordinary is that she's stopped speaking to me! And
I know her. She *won't* speak to me again until Amber and
Henry are back!

DR. OLIVER

Miss Townsend, we *can't* put Mrs. Beecham back on the
MagnaDopa because of the side effects.

SHIRLEY
(furious)
SIDE EFFECTS! ALL YOUR DRUGS HAVE SIDE
EFFECTS! AND YOU PRESCRIBE THEM ALL THE TIME!
(suddenly SHIRLEY starts slurring her words)
WHAT DOOO YOU MEANNN YOU CAN...T ...

(SHIRLEY goes limp and starts sliding out of the chair.
DR. KOMAR springs forward and catches her.)

DR. KOMAR

Miss Townsend? Can you hear me, Miss Townsend?

(SHIRLEY responds in unintelligible, slurred words.
DR. OLIVER picks up the phone and dials 911.)

DR. OLIVER

This is Dr. Oliver. I need an ambulance at the Peach Gardens
Retirement Home. NOW!

(CURTAIN)

(END OF ACT)

ACT 3

Scene 1

SETTING: Hazel's room.

AT RISE: HAZEL is getting ready to go out when AMBER emerges from the bathroom.

> AMBER

Oh, I like the new sweater, Mrs. B.

> HAZEL
> (grabbing her purse)

Thank you, Amber. I've already called the taxi so I've got to get going.

> AMBER

Taxi? Shouldn't you be getting down to breakfast?

> HAZEL

I'll get something after I feed Shirley.

> AMBER

Still no improvement, then?

HAZEL

No, not yet.

AMBER

Can she talk to you?

HAZEL

She tries, but she doesn't make any sense.

AMBER

Life's a funny thing, isn't it? A couple of weeks ago she was walking you down to breakfast and now you're feeding her.

HAZEL

It's called irony, Amber. You have to get used to it when you're old.
(on her way out the door)
By the way, would you mind not gobbling up all the Licorice Allsorts while I'm gone?

AMBER

But …

HAZEL

Don't protest. I know it's you.

AMBER
(resigned)

You say 'Hi' to Shirley for me, Mrs. B.

(AMBER heads into the bathroom.)
(HAZEL exits.)

(BLACKOUT)

(LIGHTS UP AGAIN)

(KEVIN and OFFICER WINDHAM enter.)

KEVIN
(calling out)

Mother?
(looking around)
She must have left already.

OFFICER WINDHAM

That's unfortunate.

KEVIN

She's gone to DELTACARE to feed her friend, Shirley. I don't suppose you'd care to wait?

OFFICER WINDHAM
Would you mind if I left it up to you to talk to her?

KEVIN
What should I say?

OFFICER WINDHAM
Just tell her that Victor Branch has disappeared. I'm not concerned, but I think she should be aware.

KEVIN
(annoyed)
You came all the way down here but you're not concerned? Tell me, how is it that a sociopath like that is roaming the streets in the first place?

OFFICER WINDHAM
It's just the way the system works, Mr. Beecham.

KEVIN
Not very well, you mean.

OFFICER WINDHAM
Mr. Branch has been ordered to stay away from your mother. And to come here, with all these people around, it's very unlikely he would.

KEVIN

I can't imagine how I'm going to spring this on her without getting her upset.

OFFICER WINDHAM
(ignores him and walks over
to the pull cord by the bed)
Is this a distress signal?

KEVIN

Yes, in case she needs help at night.

OFFICER WINDHAM

What about security?

KEVIN

In the building?
(OFFICER WINDHAM nods.)
I don't think there is any. No alarm system or guards, if that's what you mean.

OFFICER WINDHAM

But there's a receptionist?

KEVIN

Until 3:00 p.m.. She leaves after she sorts the mail. But there's a nurse in the clinic 24/7.

OFFICER WINDHAM

I'll have a talk with her before I leave.
(handing Kevin his card)
Have your mother call me if she has any concerns.

KEVIN

What if Victor Branch does show up?

OFFICER WINDHAM

Tell her to call 911, immediately.

KEVIN

I'm not sure how much more of this she can handle.

OFFICER WINDHAM

Confidentially, Mr. Beecham, we're all very impressed with your mother. Not many women would have gone after Branch like that in the bank.

KEVIN

But was it worth risking her life over?

OFFICER WINDHAM

I think it was more the principle of the thing. And, of course, she wanted to protect your inheritance.

KEVIN

(laughs wryly)

Officer Windham, there is no inheritance. My father gambled away every cent they had before he died.

OFFICER WINDHAM

I see. I assumed because your mother was living here ...

KEVIN

Her pension covers part of it and I make up the rest.

OFFICER WINDHAM

And you've kept this from her? Why?

KEVIN

My father had few redeeming qualities. What would be the point of adding one more disappointment to his legacy?

OFFICER WINDHAM

You're made of good stuff, Mr. Beecham. You must get it from your mother.

                    KEVIN

I must.

(BLACKOUT)

(END OF SCENE)

ACT 3

Scene 2

SETTING: SHIRLEY's room at DELTACARE Long Term Care facility. It's sparse and clinical, like a hospital room.

AT RISE: SHIRLEY is slouched in her wheelchair, dribbling porridge out of the side of her mouth as HAZEL feeds her.

HAZEL
(Talking to SHIRLEY as she
wipes the corner of her mouth.)

I think we need one of those bibs with a big trough like the infants wear.

(SHIRLEY rolls her eyes.)

Sorry.

(lifts a glass of orange juice to SHIRLEY's lips)

Try a little of this, dear. You've always liked orange juice.

(A little goes in, and comes out again. HAZEL mops it up with a napkin.)

Never mind.

(HAZEL gives up on the feeding and puts the food aside.)

Did you hear the big news from our old neighbourhood?

They're going to tear down the old hospital. Remember how

we used to rummage through the garbage cans when we were kids to see if we could find something really disgusting? (SHIRLEY just looks at her.)

They're putting up a *new* hospital beside the airport ... one of those mega things. I can't say it would put my mind at ease having one of those 747s coming down on you as you're having your bedpan changed. (HAZEL sits back, rummages through her purse for a comb and lipstick, and starts fixing SHIRLEY up. She reads the bottom of the lipstick.)

It's "Peach Perfection" today. (she smears some lipstick across SHIRLEY's limp lips then puts it back in her purse. Then she starts on her hair.)

After I leave here I'm going to have *my* hair done. Marie's doing it. Big date tonight. (SHIRLEY's eyes come alive.)

Yes, it's Henry! He's back. We're going down to the waterfront for ice cream cones. I've decided to accept him the way he is, Shirley. It's too late in life to be making a fuss about everything.

(KEVIN enters.)

KEVIN

Hello! What are my two favourite girls up to? Have we managed to get some breakfast down?

HAZEL

Not much.

(to Shirley)

But it doesn't matter at all, does it, dear?

KEVIN

Would you excuse us for a minute, Shirley?

(moves HAZEL aside)

HAZEL

I've got to get to my hair appointment, Kevin. What is it?

KEVIN

Officer Windham was just down. He wanted you to know that they can't find Victor Branch.

HAZEL
(shocked)

What? That can't be right.

KEVIN

Apparently, it is.

HAZEL

Is he going to come after me?

KEVIN

I'm sure he'd have second thoughts about going after you again, mother.

HAZEL

But what if he's afraid of what I'll say in court?

KEVIN
(impatiently)

He may be, but if you see him you're to call 911. Officer Windham has alerted the staff at the Home to be on the lookout.

HAZEL

It makes you wonder, doesn't it?

KEVIN

About what?

HAZEL

If he'd forced a child from his home and stuck a gun in his ribs, would he have gotten out on bail?
(KEVIN shrugs)
You couldn't possibly understand. You're still young. The whole system revolves around you.

KEVIN

Look, I don't have time to argue the point. I just wanted you to know. Keep your eyes open.

HAZEL
(looking at her watch)
Why don't you drop me off at the hairdresser's? It'll save me a taxi.

KEVIN

Sure, I can do that.

HAZEL
(wheels SHIRLEY over to the TV and turns it on for her)
I'll see you tomorrow, Shirley. Try not to get into trouble while I'm gone.
(to Kevin)
She loves the TODAY show.

KEVIN
(looking at his watch)
Let's fly. I'm late as it is.

(HAZEL and KEVIN exit.)

(BLACKOUT)
(END OF SCENE)

ACT 3

Scene 3

SETTING: The hairdresser's.

AT RISE: HAZEL is in the chair facing a mirror. MARIE
stands behind her with a comb in her hand. There's a manicure
table to one side.

MARIE
(combing HAZEL's hair)
Just a little off the top today, as usual?

HAZEL
(giggling)
Oh, you're such a card, Marie.

MARIE
You missed me, didn't you? I knew you would.

HAZEL
Terribly. You're the only one who can get this mop under
control.

MARIE

Looks like I'll have to take an inch off the bottom to even it out.

HAZEL

That's fine. And cut my bangs to the top of my eyebrows.

MARIE

Dry cut or shampoo?

HAZEL

Oh, shampoo, please. And an extra tip if you massage my scalp.

MARIE
(joking)
I see you haven't changed. You're just as demandin' as ever!

HAZEL

And you're just as ornery as ever!

MARIE

I guess that's what makes us a perfect match.

HAZEL

You might as well do my nails too.

MARIE
(pointing to the table)
Manicure first, then. Your nails can dry while I'm doin' your hair.

(They both move over to the manicure table. HAZEL rolls up her sleeves, slips off her ring and watch and puts them in a saucer. Then she holds out her right hand to MARIE.)

MARIE
Now look at this! You're as steady as a rock.

HAZEL
You should have seen me a week ago. They took away my medication and I was shaking like a leaf.

MARIE
Took away your medication! Are the doctors over there a bunch of noodles?

(MARIE takes HAZEL's hand and starts buffing her nails.)

HAZEL
It was all a little confusing. They were going to wait before putting me on the new medication but then they decided to do it right away. It's a good thing, too. I've got a boyfriend, you know.

MARIE

You do? Girl, we gotta lot of catchin' up to do.

HAZEL

I bet you thought I was just over there playing bingo and watching Wheel of Fortune.

MARIE
(laughing)
You're just a little mindreader today, aren't you?

HAZEL

Did you hear about Shirley? She had another stroke.

MARIE

Yes, I did. How's she doin'?

HAZEL

She's at Long Term Care now. They wouldn't let her stay at the Home.

MARIE

Oh dear. She doesn't deserve that.

HAZEL

They keep telling me there's hope, but I think that's just to make me feel better.

MARIE

Oh, I don't know. The preacher at the Baptist Church had a stroke a year ago and he's as fit as a fiddle now.

HAZEL
(skeptical)
I don't think Shirley's ever going to be fit as a fiddle.

MARIE
(She shows HAZEL the colour chart to change the subject.)
What shade would madame like today?

HAZEL
(looking them over carefully)
How about this one?

MARIE

Honey, that is Flame Red! Are you tryin' to get that man of yours all worked up?

HAZEL

It's not that, Marie. I need something bold. Something that says, "Don't mess with me".

MARIE

You got someone messin' with you?

HAZEL

Yes. That scoundrel that abducted me!

MARIE

But that was months ago! Haven't they locked him up and thrown away the key?

HAZEL

Not yet.

MARIE

In that case, I'm putting on an extra coat, for courage.

HAZEL
(solemn)

Yes, for courage.

MARIE
(putting a dish of sudsy water in front of HAZEL)

Now, let's soften up those cuticles and forget all about that villain. You just tell me about that fella of yours.

(BLACKOUT)

(END OF SCENE)

ACT 3

Scene 4

SETTING: HAZEL's room.

AT RISE: HENRY and HAZEL are dancing to music. HAZEL looks at HENRY, hardly believing he's there.

HAZEL

I'm glad you like dancing, Henry.

HENRY
(chuckling)
It's really a ploy to get close to you, my darling.

HAZEL

I used to dance a lot when I was in high school. Usually in someone's basement on a Saturday night.

HENRY

That's where I learned! I was a popular partner because the other boys weren't interested.

HAZEL

My husband, George, wasn't interested. The only time he ever danced was at our wedding. And only then because it was expected.

HENRY

I wonder what George is up to now.

HAZEL

George is dead.

HENRY

I know. But that doesn't mean he isn't up to something.

HAZEL

In heaven, you mean, if that's where he is. If he has a whiskey and a deck of cards, I'm sure he's in heaven.

HENRY

He liked his drink then, did he?

HAZEL

Yes. He was very much like you in that respect.

HENRY

And you didn't like it?

HAZEL

I think a cocktail or two before dinner is fine. But George's drinking was different. If he didn't drink a certain quota every day he ...

HENRY

He what?

HAZEL

He couldn't function. Of course, he didn't function very well regardless, but *he* didn't know that.

HENRY

You've never talked about this with me. Who do you confide in?

HAZEL

Only Shirley.

HENRY

Well, I'm glad you told me.

HAZEL

Shirley thought I should so you'd understand why I jumped on you about the Bailey's. But, I've made my peace with it. I can't change you. There's not even enough time to change me.

HENRY

You notice it too, do you? That there's so little time left?

HAZEL

Doesn't everybody? Do you ever wonder what it's going to be like at the end, when you're slipping away?

HENRY

I imagine it's like letting go of a hand and falling into space.

HAZEL

But where do you land?

HENRY

I'm not sure. Maybe you just keep travelling through space.

HAZEL

Or become a star.

HENRY

Well, if I get bored I might consider it.
(HAZEL laughs)

(knock at the door)

HAZEL

Good heavens! Who can that be?
(breaks from HENRY's embrace and turns off the music)

HENRY

You want me to hide?

HAZEL

Would you mind? It might be the nurse.
(HENRY disappears into the bathroom. HAZEL is about to
open the door when it is flung open rather violently, almost
knocking her down. VICTOR rushes in menacingly and closes
the door behind him.)
You!

VICTOR

I thought you might remember me.

HAZEL
(backing up)

What do you want?

VICTOR

Now that's the right question, isn't it? What do you think I
want?

HAZEL

If I were you, I'd want to stay out of jail. Maybe you should
have thought about that before you pulled a gun on me.

VICTOR
(smacking her across the face)
You've got a smart mouth on you, don't you?
(HAZEL is reeling, holding her hand up to her face.)
You old ladies are all the same!

HAZEL
(screaming at the top of her lungs)
HENRY! HELP ME, HENRY! HELP!

(VICTOR looks around, startled.)

VICTOR

You got someone in here, old lady?

(HENRY emerges from the bathroom.)

HAZEL

There you are, Henry! Tell me what to do!

VICTOR

(Looks where HAZEL is looking and is completely mystified.)
Lady, you think *I've* got problems? You're a raving nutcase!

HENRY

Don't whimper, Hazel. Stand up to him.

HAZEL
(angrily)

What did you call me?

VICTOR

Why? Are you hard of hearing too?

HENRY

Atta girl, Hazel. Give it to him.

HAZEL
(raising her voice)

You think *I'm* the stupid one? You're the one going to jail.

VICTOR

What?

HAZEL
(getting revved up)

Tell me, how do you justify beating up little old ladies? Do you blame it on a tragic childhood? Were you misunderstood?

VICTOR

Don't give me all that psychobabble horseshit.

HAZEL
(bolder)
Why don't we discuss it over a cup of tea? You can tell me
your story and I'll tell you mine and we'll see whose childhood
was the worst.

VICTOR
(coming toward her)
Let's talk about you keeping your big trap shut! Or do I have to
shut it permanently?
(spins her so that he's behind her, holding his arm across her
neck)

HAZEL
(shouting desperately, as Victor strengthens his grip)
HELP HENRY! HELP!

VICTOR
I don't think that Henry dude is coming to help you, bitch.

HENRY
Do what I say, Hazel and you'll be all right.

HAZEL
I will?

VICTOR

You will what?

HENRY

BITE DOWN ON HIS ARM AS HARD AS YOU CAN,
HAZEL! NOW!
(HAZEL bites down on VICTOR. He screams and releases his
grip.)
NOW, TWIST AND GIVE HIM A KNEE TO THE GROIN!
(HAZEL turns to face VICTOR and knees him.
He falls forward, groaning and clutching himself.)
NOW, RUN, HAZEL! RUN!

(HAZEL runs for the door screaming at the top of her
lungs. The door flies open and the NURSE is standing
there with a baseball bat in her hands. She catches
HAZEL on the fly.)

NURSE

I've got you, Mrs. Beecham. The police are on their way …
(eyeing VICTOR BRANCH writhing on the floor)
… although it looks like you've got everything under control.

HAZEL
(breathless)
How did you know he was here?

NURSE

Are you kidding? All the bedside alarms in this wing are going off! Are you okay?

HAZEL
(feeling her cheek where he smacked her)
Yes, I think so.

NURSE

Why don't you go down to the lounge and relax, honey? I'll take care of things here.

HAZEL

I ... I have a guest. I don't think I should leave him.

NURSE
(knowingly)
He's welcome to go with you. The coffee machine's still on.

HAZEL

All right, then. Come along, Henry.

(HENRY walks over and takes HAZEL's hand.)

HENRY

That was good work, dear. You nailed him.

HAZEL

I did, didn't I?

(HAZEL and HENRY exit holding hands. A police
siren is heard in the distance.)

(VICTOR starts to stir. NURSE moves closer to him
and raises the bat.)

NURSE

Go ahead. Give me a reason.

(BLACKOUT)

(END OF SCENE)

ACT 3

Scene 5

SETTING: A park-like setting outside the DELTACARE Long Term Care facility.
It is now fall.

AT RISE: HAZEL is sitting on a park bench. SHIRLEY is in her wheelchair. They're finishing a couple of sandwiches that HAZEL had wrapped in waxed paper.

HAZEL

Just what I had in the cupboard: peanut butter and honey. Remember how we'd trade sandwiches at school and you'd always want my peanut butter and honey?

SHIRLEY
(nods)

Ah-hum.

HAZEL

Personally I don't like the way the peanut butter sticks to the roof of my mouth.

SHIRLEY
(smiles)

I do.

HAZEL

Did I tell you about Maxine, the new lady at my table? You'd like her. She's bright and bubbly, and she's still with it. Oh, I don't mean you aren't. I know you are, Shirley. You're coming back.
(SHIRLEY gives her a thumbs-up.)
I want to tell you about Maxine though, because she's so unique. She keeps all of us in stitches with jokes she gets off the internet. I wish I could remember them. Maybe she'd print them out so that I could bring them over. You'd get a kick out of them. And, are you ready for this? She's got me going down to cards twice a week! There's a group of us. They're very nice ladies.

(They finish their sandwiches and HAZEL brushes the crumbs from their laps. Then she neatly folds the waxed paper and slips it into her purse.)

SHIRLEY

Amber?

HAZEL

Amber? Oh, I thought I told you. She got through her
community service and is going on to get her high school
diploma. I never doubted it, did I, Shirley? Something's going
to come of that girl.

(She spots the aide.)

Uh, oh. Carlos is coming.

(SHIRLEY'S eyes follow hers.)

(CARLOS enters.)

CARLOS

Hello, ladies. I see you're enjoying this beautiful day.

HAZEL

Yes, we are.

CARLOS

Sorry to break up your little party but Miss Townsend has an
appointment in Physio.

HAZEL

That's quite all right. Tell them whatever they're doing down
there, it's working.

CARLOS

Ain't that the truth? Pretty soon she'll be chasing me around
the hallways!

(SHIRLEY grimaces and rolls her eyes, mirthfully.)

HAZEL

Well, you two run along.

(CARLOS wheels SHIRLEY off.)
(KEVIN passes them on his way in.)

KEVIN

Hello Shirley. Goodbye Shirley.
(SHIRLEY gives him a little wave.)
Wow, she's really improving.

HAZEL

It'll take more than a little stroke to finish Shirley off.

KEVIN

I think you can take some credit for her recovery, mother. If
you hadn't been down here taking care of her, she might have
starved to death.

HAZEL

What was I supposed to do, Kevin? Let her sit in wet diapers
all day, sipping Ensure through a straw? They just don't have
the staff.

KEVIN

Well, you really stepped up when she needed you.
(looking at his watch)
Now, I'm afraid, you've got to step up one more time.

HAZEL
(squaring her shoulders)
I'm ready.

KEVIN

Did you remember your Victim Impact Statement?

HAZEL
(opens her purse and pulls it out)
Right here. I hope they throw the book at him.

KEVIN

I don't think it's going to be a life sentence, mother.

HAZEL

Still.

KEVIN

What about Henry? Is he coming?

HAZEL
(looks at him peculiarly)
Henry? Why, Henry's gone to Japan!

KEVIN
Japan? You didn't tell me.

HAZEL
I thought I had.

KEVIN
Did you two have a spat?

HAZEL
No. It was just obvious that Shirley needed me more. I told him what my priorities were and he was very understanding. Turns out he'd been thinking about going on a trip for some time.

KEVIN
Speaking of trips, mother, I got the bill for your taxis today. I think I'm going to have to buy you a bicycle.

HAZEL
(putting her arm in his as they stroll off)
Not to worry, Kevin. I took a hundred dollars off the ladies at poker last night.

KEVIN
(stops and looks at her in surprise)
Since when do you play poker?

HAZEL
Since I met Maxine. She's the new lady at my table.

KEVIN
When you say "took", you mean you won it, right?

HAZEL
I do?

KEVIN
(alarmed)
Mother!

HAZEL
(laughing)
Honestly, Kevin, someday your face is going to freeze like that.
LOL.

(CURTAIN)

(END OF PLAY)

Breakfast in the Garden, Giuseppe de Nittis, 1883

He painted himself as an empty chair.
The mind's eye a photograph.
The last flash behind his eyelids
as he lay dying.

A wife, a son, dressed for breakfast.
China, sterling, sugar cubes,
a spoon dunk in tea.
The last beautiful scene of his life.
The legacy of his brush.

The Island of the Dead, Arnold Böcklin, 1886

It cut an imposing figure on the lake -

the slabbed-stone fortress that inspired the Führer

to erect fortified concrete on cliffs

to mow down armies breaching the beaches.

Hapless soldiers lost to the priest.

The boatman rowing into the tunnel of death,

oars as regular as a heart muscle

slapping out a beat.

the exact likeness of living persons

The power was intermittent for a week
before it quit altogether -
    transformers drowned in a hurricane
    spawned in the boiling waters of the Gulf.

Charging stations across the state
cradle their dead cell babies
    while monster appliances
    in matching stainless
    foul themselves.

The cereal was devoured heedlessly
when food aid was promised
to curb the hunger.
    Now the cupboard is bare and
    scrawny scavengers push through
the malodorous muck of maggoty dumpsters
hunting for a bag of chips
or an overlooked chocolate bar
    to feed feverish parents
    befuddled in their beds.

When the ground begins to quake
they scramble out of the bin
wide-eyed at the relief convoy of refrigerated trucks
grinding down the swampy street
    like an articulated caterpillar
    running apathetic stoplights.

The wretched waifs run to catch up
as a hunger-crazed mob armed with bats and shovels
blockades the caravan. Drags out the drivers.
      Beats them senseless.
      Bloody as steaks.

Sweat-soaked men wrestle the doors
prepared to shove each other aside
      for armloads
      of milk and juice and meat
until the trucks reveal their unexpected bounty:
colonies of white cocoons
bound and stuffed in the quiet coolness
      preserved for burial in derelict plantations
      sectioned like quilts into muddy trenches.

Faces masked only by disappointment
hesitate and blink at the scene before them,
desperation driving their brains
to contemplate the actual state of decomposition,
calculating the math of edibleness
if they excise the plague-riddled organs
      and serve up the muscles
      thinly-sliced with wasabi,
      or barbecued with sauce
      left over in the fridge.

A phalanx of cop cars interrupts them.
Riotous faces contort with rage
and SHOUT their defiance
at the presumption
    that they can be controlled,
    their rights violated.

Officers pop open their trunks and
shoulder their rifles
    as the mass swarms them
    with the suffocating ferocity
    of a Gulf wave.

The children watch from the curb,
breathless with anticipation
as the spectacle unfolds.
    Sharing a bunch
    of black bananas.
    Turning to soup in their skins.

Just To Get It Straight

Verse #1

We love the same boy.

He's in both our hearts.

He's chasing me and I'm chasing you.

Wondering what I can do.

Chorus:

How'd it come to this?

You won't look at me.

How'd it come to this?

You won't talk to me.

Now you're telling everyone that's on me.

Just to get it straight

I'm not going to wait

Cuz I love him - but I miss you.

Verse #2

I'm stuck on the line I drew

Something I never meant to do.

Don't blame me for loving him

the way I do. I never meant to.

Chorus:

How'd it come to this?

You won't look at me.

How'd it come to this?

You won't talk to me.

Now you're telling everyone that's on me.

Just to get it straight

I'm not going to wait

Cuz I love him - but I miss you.

Verse #3

I'm not giving myself away

Don't think of it that way

Choosing between him and you

Is not hard for me to do

Chorus:

How'd it come to this?

You won't look at me.

How'd it come to this?

You won't talk to me.

Now you're telling everyone that's on me.

Just to get it straight

I'm not going to wait
Cuz I love him - but I miss you.

Verse #4

You can't see me standing here
Because you're trying to disappear.
You know that he picked me.
Do you know that I picked you?

Chorus:

How'd it come to this?
You won't look at me.
How'd it come to this?
You won't talk to me.
Now you're telling everyone that's on me.
Just to get it straight
I'm not going to wait
Cuz I love him - but I miss you.

Just to get it straight
I'm not going to wait
Cuz I love him - but I miss you.

About the Author

Margaret J. McMaster published her first book of middle-grade fiction, **Carried Away on Licorice Days**, in 2008. It was nominated for three literary awards: the Canadian Library Association's Book of the Year for Children Award, the 2010/2011 Hackmatack Children's Choice Book Award, and the 2011 Rocky Mountain Book Award. In 2009 she started writing the *Babysitter Out of Control!* series. These amusing, fast-paced adventures include: **Babysitter Out of Control!**, **Looking for Love on Mongo Tongo, The Improbable Party on Purple Plum Lane, What Happened in July**, **The Sinking of the Wiley Bean,** and, **The Queen of Second Chances. The Complete Babysitter Out of Control! Series**, published in 2015, was long-listed for the 2016 Silver Birch Award, was a *Best Books for Kids & Teens* selection, and won the GOLD MEDAL in the *2015 Moonbeam Children's Book Award, Early Reader/1st Chapter Books* category. McMaster is a past contributor to the *Canadian Children's Annual* and her creative non-fiction piece, *After All These Years,* was shortlisted for the 2006 CBC Literary Award. **So Much Potential**, a novel set in the Lake Erie fishing industry, was published in 2013. It was a *Best Book for Kids & Teens *Starred* Selection.* The first book in her Phoebe Sproule series, **8 Days in DUMBO**, was named one of *The Year's Best* by *Resource Links* and won an Honourable Mention in the 2019/2020 Reader Views Literary Awards. The sequel, **The Haunting of Cedar Hill Plantation**, was released in 2020 and won a Bronze Medal in the Reader Views Literary Awards.

BOOKS by THIS AUTHOR

Teen Fiction:
So Much Potential

Juvenile Fiction:
The Haunting of Cedar Hill Plantation
8 Days in DUMBO
Carried Away on Licorice Days

Early Chapter Books:
Babysitter Out of Control!
Looking For Love on Mongo Tongo
The Improbable Party on Purple Plum Lane
What Happened in July
The Sinking of the Wiley Bean
The Queen of Second Chances
The Complete Babysitter Out of Control! Series

Owen isn't expecting anything other than a good night's sleep when he's shipped off to his grandmother's farm after his baby sister is born, but he soon discovers that he fits right in with the three-legged dog, the blind goat, and a very angry pony. Then Grandma wins the lottery and everything changes.

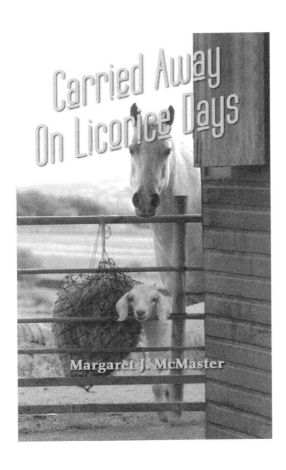

Carried Away
On Licorice Days

Margaret J. McMaster

12-year-old Phoebe Sproule may be embarrassed by her mother's blog *(featuring every laughable fact of her existence!)* but its 2 million followers prove useful in solving the mystery of Peter Philby's disappearance from the Starbrite Diner in Brooklyn.

It's supposed to be a summer getaway at her relatives' plantation in Nashville but Phoebe quickly discovers that her cousin Baxter is desperate to find a treasure hidden during the Civil War and his sister Rachel's relationship with her boyfriend is on the rocks. Underneath it all is a plantation that hasn't put its past to rest, and the aftermath of a deadly tornado is about to reveal the truth.

Andy Towell's dream of becoming a commercial
fisherman is jeopardized when a co-worker goes missing.

Margaret J. McMaster

SO MUCH

POTENTIAL

The zany adventures of Stewart and his eccentric babysitter, Mrs. Chairbottom, are featured in this compilation of the six books in the Babysitter Out of Control! series: **Babysitter Out of Control!**, **Looking for Love on Mongo Tongo**, **The Improbable Party on Purple Plum Lane**, **What Happened in July**, **The Sinking of the Wiley Bean**, and, **The Queen of Second Chances.**

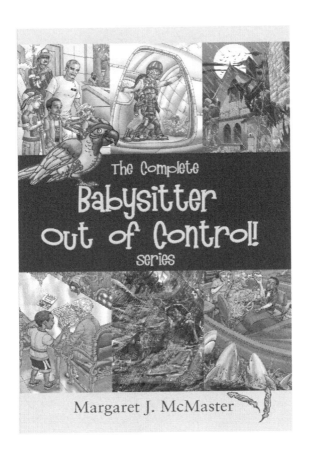

Manufactured by Amazon.ca
Bolton, ON

30049138R00141